PAYBACK
on
POPLAR
LANE

by
MARGARET MINCKS

PUFFIN BOOKS

PUFFIN BOOKS
An imprint of Penguin Random House LLC
375 Hudson Street
New York, New York 10014

First published in the United States of America by Viking,
an imprint of Penguin Random House LLC, 2018
Published by Puffin Books, an imprint of Penguin Random House LLC, 2019

THE LIBRARY OF CONGRESS HAS CATALOGED THE VIKING EDITION AS FOLLOWS:
Names: Mincks, Margaret, author.
Title: Payback on Poplar Lane / by Margaret Mincks.
Description: New York: Viking, [2018] | Series: Poplar kids ; 1 | Summary: A
friendly neighborhood business competition between sixth-graders Rachel
Chambers, so quiet she is practically invisible, and Peter S. Gronkowski,
future mogul, turns into a ruthless rivalry.
Identifiers: LCCN 2017033434 | ISBN 9780425290903 (hardcover)
Subjects: | CYAC: Entrepreneurship—Fiction. | Competition
(Psychology)—Fiction. | Neighborhoods—Fiction.
Classification: LCC PZ7.1.M6315 Pay 2018 | DDC [Fic]—dc23
LC record available at https://lccn.loc.gov/2017033434

Puffin Books ISBN 9780425290910

Book design by Nancy Brennan
Printed in the United States of America

1   3   5   7   9   10   8   6   4   2

For Scott and Mattie

NOTICE OF SILENT PERIOD

Dear Poplar Lane,

Thank you for supporting my extremely successful business, Star Maps of Poplar Lane. It's been a pleasure making high-quality maps starring you, the fine citizens of our cul-de-sac. I've learned so much about your lives, careers, and square footages.

As my mentor Tom Reddi once said, part of being great at business is knowing when to move on. So I've decided to sunset Star Maps of Poplar Lane. That means I'm not doing it anymore.

Don't worry. This isn't good-bye forever. I'm taking a silent period of one week to cook up my next big project.

It's a recipe for success. Add the can-do attitude of Peter's U-Inflate Self-Service Tire Pump, the artistic flair of Peter's Porch Selfie Station, and the streetwise sophistication of Uber-Peter's Textbook Transport Wagon. Put them in a business blender. Makes one serving of my next smash hit.

Fortunately yours,

Peter S. Gronkowski

Founder, CEO, CFO, and COO of Peter Presents, Inc.

P.S. You are cordially invited to attend my corporate launch party next Friday at 4 p.m. It's in my garage. I predict there will be a huge announcement about an exciting business opportunity just for you. This is your chance to be a leader. Don't miss out.

P.P.S. Yes, there will be Peter Presents, Inc., Cupcakes.

P.P.P.S. No, there will not be lemonade. Business tip: Lemonade is for amateurs.

Be Yourself!

Poplar Lane Middle School
"Self"-Ebration Self-Portrait Contest

INSTRUCTIONS: Show Us Who You Really Are! Draw a Self-Portrait Below.

PRIZES: Winner will receive a coupon for one Mega Freezy Shake at the Cone Zone (limit one topping), his/her picture on the front page of the *Poplar Middle School Daily Chronicle*, and membership in Poplar Middle School's Random Acts of Artness Club. Winner will also reveal their self-portrait and address the school board at the next Poplar County School Board meeting.

IT'S YOUR TURN!

NAME: Rachel Chambers

TELL US ABOUT YOURSELF: A picture is worth a thousand words (that's what my dad says).

DRAW YOUR SELF-PORTRAIT HERE:

1

Rachel

I peeked outside my house to make sure no one was looking. On this cul-de-sac, someone is usually looking.

The path to the mailbox was clear, so I tiptoed over. Inside was a smooshed construction-paper cat sculpture and a thin white envelope with my name on it. I knew what it was: the results of the Poplar Middle School Self-Portrait Contest.

Boom, boom, boom!

My best friend, Clover, banged on her bedroom window. She lives across the street.

"I got my letter, too! I'll call you!" Clover yelled. Her voice was crystal clear even though the window was shut. Dr. Spumoni says Clover has excessive earwax. Unless she gets the wax flushed out once a month, she can't hear herself talk.

Dad says Clover and I are best friends because opposites attract. She's obsessed with cats. I like dogs, and my earwax is fine. We're like two peas in a pod, but the pod is kind of warped and uneven. I'm the smaller, quieter pea.

I hurried inside and answered the phone.

"Eeeeee!" Clover squealed. "Let's find out at exactly the same time. One, two—I won!" she said just as I was unfolding my letter.

DISQUALIFIED. The word screamed at me in thick red marker, right on top of my drawing. THIS IS NOT A SELF-PORTRAIT. IT'S A TURTLE.

"I . . . didn't," I said. My face felt numb. There was something extra pathetic about being disqualified from a self-portrait contest.

I read the directions again: *Show us who you really are! Draw a self-portrait below.* They never said you couldn't see yourself as a turtle.

I'm not the only one who thinks I'm a turtle. At the last parent-teacher conference, Mrs. Francis told Dad I needed to come out of my shell. Why? The world is noisy enough. Maybe more people should stay in their shells.

"Oh no!" Clover said. She sounded horrified, like it never occurred to her that if she won, someone else would have to lose.

Clover always wins. She wins so much that I'm her official victory speechwriter. It's practically a full-time job.

"It's okay," I said. "I like the cat sculpture." Clover makes me a new piece of animal art every week. Most of the time it's a cat.

"Thanks! I'm experimenting with glitter," Clover said. She's always experimenting with glitter. "Anyway . . . cupcakes!"

"What cupcakes?"

"Peter's party. Didn't you get the invitation?"

I didn't say anything.

"Oh," Clover said. She stayed quiet for one whole second. "I bet he meant to—"

"It's okay," I said. Sometimes I say things are okay without even thinking about whether it's true.

Peter Gronkowski had been my next-door neighbor for our entire lives, and he still didn't know I existed. It's hard for people to remember you when you have a best friend like Clover.

"Come to the party with me," Clover said. "You can be my date!"

I sighed. "Okay," I said. If I didn't go, Dad would probably make me read a book on engaging with my peers.

"Oh! I have to give a speech for the contest," Clover said. "Can you help me?"

"I'm kind of . . . busy," I said. "But I guess so."

"Thanks, Rach!" Clover squealed. I held the phone away from my ear. "You're the be-e-e-e-e-st!" *Click.*

Dad says I'm like a guy in an old play called *Cyrano de Bergerac.* Cyrano was a really good writer, but his friend got all the credit because he said Cyrano's words out loud.

One time I Googled Cyrano de Bergerac. He had a gigantic nose (ew) and was in love with his cousin (double ew). Does that sound like a compliment to you?

The reason I'm kind of busy is a secret. It's such a big secret that not even Clover knows. The only person who knows is not a person. (It's my dog, Molly.)

My secret is that I'm writing a book called *Cyrano's Revenge.* In my book, Cyrano is a girl with an average nose. She's tired of only helping other people. She wants to shine on her own.

Just because I'm quiet doesn't mean I don't have anything to say.

There were three signs on Peter Gronkowski's front lawn. One said LAUNCH PARTY THIS WAY with an arrow pointing to his garage. The second was a picture of a rocket with a caption that said 5, 4, 3, 2, 1 . . . COUNTDOWN TO SUCCESS! The third was a drawing of a lemonade pitcher with a red X through it.

"What do you think Peter's new business is?" Clover asked as we walked into his garage.

"An alien-human student exchange program?" I guessed.

"Ahahahahahahaha!" Clover's laugh bounced all over the garage walls. One good thing about having a loud best friend is that she laughs extra hard at your jokes.

Making jokes is one of my secret talents. I only make jokes with Clover, Molly, and Dad. Once Clover told Mrs. Francis I was funny, and Mrs. Francis laughed because she thought *that* was a joke.

Peter's garage was already packed with kids from the cul-de-sac. Most were crowded around the Peter Presents, Inc., Cupcake Tower. The PP frosting logo on each cupcake was starting to melt, so the display was looking a little slimy. A big sign read PETER

PRESENTS, INC., CUPCAKES: TO BE EATEN ONLY AFTER THE HUGE ANNOUNCEMENT AND ONLY IF YOU HAVE A GREEN WRISTBAND. BEST, PETER GRONKOWSKI, FOUNDER, CEO, COO, AND CFO.

"Droooool," said Clover. "Peter's mom is a cupcake genius."

"Yeah," I said. But I could see Mr. Gronkowski through the door at the top of the garage stairs. He was wearing a white apron with chocolate stains on it. And Mrs. Gronkowski was at work.

Conclusion: Mr. Gronkowski was the cupcake genius.

Before I could tell Clover my theory, Ken Spumoni ran over. He was wearing a black T-shirt that said SECURITY.

"Hey, Clover!" Ken said. "Don't forget to write your essay." He pointed at a crystal ball with a sign beside it that said PETER PRESENTS, INC., CRYSTAL BALL OF OPPORTUNITY. ONE ESSAY = ONE CUPCAKE.

"Essay?" Clover asked. She wrinkled her nose. "Like school?"

"Not really," Ken said. He looked down at his clipboard. "The topic is, 'Why do you want to work for Peter Gronkowski?'"

"I don't," Clover said.

"Do you want a cupcake?" he asked.

"Yeah," she replied.

Ken shrugged.

"But I'm an artist," Clover said. "Not a writer. Not like Rachel."

Ken scrunched his eyebrows like he was thinking hard. "Who?" he asked. Then, finally, he spotted me. "Oh, Puppet! I didn't see you there."

I felt like an ant at somebody's romantic picnic.

For the record, I never asked to be called Puppet, obviously. But that annoying nickname has stuck like glue since the beginning of the school year.

The whole class was "encouraged" (forced) to audition for *The Wizard of Oz, Junior.* Being onstage is my living nightmare, but I had no choice.

Mr. Hodges, the piano teacher, said it was my turn. He started playing the Cowardly Lion's song, "If I Were King of the Forest." When I opened my mouth to sing, nothing came out. I froze like a block of ice.

Clover thought I'd forgotten the words. She started singing to help me out. But my mouth was hanging open, so it looked like I was singing with her voice.

Clover got the part of Dorothy. I got Girl Handing Out Programs in the Lobby.

After that, kids started calling me Puppet (if they called me anything at all). I didn't even raise my hand in class anymore. Whenever I did, someone would make a "creaky" sound, which was supposed to be the sound of puppet strings. Then everyone would laugh.

"She's not Puppet," Clover told Ken. "She's Rachel!" Clover grabbed a piece of paper and an orange pen. "Fine, I'll do a picture essay."

Clover hates my nickname, too, but she still talks for me all the time. I must look like a wounded animal when I'm thinking of what to say, so she probably figures she's putting me out of my misery.

Sometimes it's nice. But mostly I wish she would stop.

"Pup—I mean, here you go," Ken said, handing me paper and a purple pen.

I stared at the blank page. I imagined DISQUALIFIED stamped over anything I wrote.

What if I didn't get disqualified, though? What if I won? That could be even worse, because I might have to give a speech. I'd freeze onstage just like I did at my audition.

But maybe not. Maybe I'd surprise everyone with my confident and amazing speaking skills.

Who was I kidding? I gave the paper and pen back to Ken without writing a word.

"Rachel's not a big contest person," Clover explained.

She would probably win, anyway. And I bet she wouldn't be disqualified, even though she was drawing a picture for an essay contest.

"What's Peter's new business?" Clover asked as she dropped her entry into the crystal ball. She winked at me. "An alien-student exchange program?"

Ken snorted. "Good one."

I waited for Clover to tell Ken that was *my* joke, but she didn't. He wouldn't have believed it anyway.

Ken gave Clover a green wristband. "This will get you one cupcake," he said.

The door at the top of the stairs swung wide open. Peter's little brother, Daniel, ran out.

"The Amazing Peter is on his way!" Daniel yelled.

He slammed the door behind him and ran down the stairs, nearly tripping over his superhero cape. He pressed a button on a fancy speaker, and spooky Halloween music filled the garage.

But it's March, I thought.

The door opened again, this time very slowly. And there he was.

Peter Gronkowski.

The crowd went quiet (even Clover). For a few seconds, Peter just stood at the top of the stairs. He came down slowly, one step at a time, like a king before his subjects.

Peter wore a bathrobe with a T-shirt wrapped around his head like a turban. Most kids would never wear something like that. But for Peter, the more embarrassing the outfit, the cooler he looked.

He walked onstage and stopped in the middle like he owned the room. I guess he kind of did, because it was his garage. Still, I felt dizzy, like his confidence sucked up all the air.

Kids jostled to the front to get closer, like hungry fish fighting for chum. I held tight to Clover's sleeve, more like a barnacle.

Being ignored hurts. Not just your feelings, but also your toes. People can crush them when they don't see you. When you're small you somehow feel like you're always in the way, which doesn't make sense. Small people take up less space. But as small as I am, I always seem to be shrinking. I'm afraid one day I'll disappear.

The Halloween music stopped.

"Welcome!" Peter said. "It's my great privilege to announce the launch of my new business: Fabulous Fortunes."

As he talked, he took gigantic steps back and forth across the stage.

Peter Gronkowski was no barnacle. He was a great white shark, ruling the ocean.

I couldn't breathe, and not just because J. J. Roma's elbow was blocking my nostrils.

Entering Peter's contest was something I had to try, for my own survival. If not, I could get washed away, and I think I'd rather swim.

I let go of Clover's sleeve and tiptoed to the Crystal Ball of Opportunity.

"I want to write an essay," I whispered to Ken. He stared at Peter onstage like he was in a trance.

I cleared my throat. Nothing.

"Ahem!" I said again.

Ken jumped. So did I. "Huh?" he said.

"I want to work for Peter Gronkowski."

2
PETER

 BUSINESS TIP: To achieve success, you must first Visualize it.

Visualizing means you picture something in your head before it happens. I learned about Visualizing from my mentor, successful local businessman Tom Reddi. It was in his monthly magazine, *Mind Your Business*. I'm a loyal subscriber.

I closed my eyes and Visualized a highly successful launch party for my new business: Fabulous Fortunes. I Felt the breeze of dollar bills waving in my face. I Smelled sweat and stress-activated cinnamon deodorant as kids shoved closer to the stage. I Heard—

"Swish," my brother, Daniel, said. "Swish."

I opened my left eye. "Visualizing is silent," I said.

"Oh," he said.

I re-Visualized. I Heard the crowd chanting "Peter Rules." I Tasted my post-party Success Snack: one Little Buster's double fudge brownie and an ice-cold glass of 2 percent milk. I—

"I flew, Peter!" Daniel said. "I saw it in my brain!" He hopped up and ran around the kitchen table, his cape streaming behind him.

Dad wiped his hands on his apron. "Great job, Danny Boy!" he said. They high-fived.

I sighed.

Daniel is four. He has a lot to learn about Visualizing. Dad is forty. He should know better.

 BUSINESS TIP: Being a big brother is like being a boss.

First, you're responsible for someone's personal and professional growth. Second, you get to tell them what to do.

Daniel hugged Dad around his chocolate-covered knees. "I like when you stay home from work!" Daniel said.

I cleared my throat.

BUSINESS TIP: Employees don't need to know everything.

Daniel needs to know that professionals walk and don't run. That leaders don't chew with their mouths open.

He doesn't need to know that Dad got laid off.

Tom Reddi says knowing everything confuses people. It makes them uncooperative, unproductive, and unpredictable. Emotional. I'm a CEO. Emotions are not part of my skill set.

I checked my watch. 3:57 p.m.

"It's time," I told Daniel. I patted him on the back. "Remember: be professional. You can do it."

I opened the door, staying out of my future customers' sight.

"Swish!" Daniel yelled. He ran past me and barged down the stairs.

 BUSINESS TIP: You can only control yourself and your reactions.

I shut the door behind him.

Just as I started my ten Rejuvenating Jumping Jacks, Dad put his hand on my shoulder. He smelled like vanilla.

"Hope they like the cupcakes," he said.

 BUSINESS TIP: People who get laid off need encouragement.

Laid off doesn't mean fired. Tom Reddi says when you're laid off, it's not your fault. It's in the "Laid Off but Not Lying Down" issue of *Mind Your Business*. When someone loses their job, you're not supposed to ask what happened. Ask practical things ("When is your next interview?") and give helpful advice ("Update your résumé with marketable skills.").

"The frosting looks professional," I said. "Almost as good as the cupcakes at the Cone Zone." I wouldn't usually encourage Dad's baking habit. It's time he could spend job-searching. But he needed encouragement. And my launch parties needed cupcakes. That's a win-win situation.

Music from my "Failure Is Frightening" playlist flowed through the crack under the door. It's the perfect playlist for Fabulous Fortunes. First, scary music is on-brand with fortune-telling. Second, fear is a great motivator for action.

"Go get 'em," Dad said.

I nodded. Part of my job as a leader is putting out

fires. Dad getting laid off is a big fire. But Fabulous Fortunes was a hose.

One, two, three. I opened the door.

Showtime.

"Welcome!" I said. "It's my great privilege to announce the launch of my new business: Fabulous Fortunes."

Half of my future customers stared at me. The other half stared at the Peter Presents, Inc., Cupcake Tower.

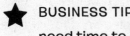 **BUSINESS TIP: Be patient. People need time to process brilliance.**

"Yay, Peter!" Daniel yelled. He charged the stage with his arms stretched out.

 BUSINESS TIP: Everything is negotiable.

That includes hugs. Every night, I hug Daniel after we read bedtime articles from *Mind Your Business*. But I don't allow hugs in the workplace.

I held up one hand to stop Daniel and stuck out my other hand. He grabbed it. We pulled in together for a one-handed hug and back slap. That's the Corporate Handshake. I learned it from my second mentor, Granddad Gronkowski. He said the Corporate Handshake sends a message: "I like you, but let's keep things professional."

I checked my watch. 4:41 p.m. The watch is solid gold. The engraving on the back says, TIME IS MONEY. BDG. BDG are Granddad's initials. He told me everything should be monogrammed. A monogram is your brand. Putting your brand on something says, "This is mine." It also says, "This is me."

Granddad gave me his watch before he died last summer. It's the official timepiece of Peter Presents, Inc.

"I know this is a lot to take in," I reassured the crowd. "The floor is now open for questions."

Mel Chang raised her hand.

 BUSINESS TIP: People are like machines—predictable. Study their patterns.

Mel is always first. She has to be. Her blog is about trends.

"Mel Chang, Poplar Lane blogger," she said. Mel always introduces herself at media events. That's how I know she's a real professional. She held up her Charming Copper Atlas 6.0 phone like a recorder. "Can you tell us more about Fabulous Fortunes?"

"Certainly," I said. Mel Chang is an IR: Important Relationship.

 BUSINESS TIP: Invest in IRs.

Businesses live and die by Mel's one-through-five-star reviews. Of course I've never gotten less than a five. "Fabulous Fortunes is all about quality fortune-telling. By me. I'm a master fortune-teller."

"Peter can see the future!" yelled Daniel.

 BUSINESS TIP: Yelling is not professional.

"Perf," said Mel. That means "perfect." Mel makes words shorter. It's part of her brand.

"A fortune-teller?" Clover O'Reilly said. "That's sooooo cool!"

Clover is not an IR like Mel Chang. I wouldn't take Clover mini-golfing or buy her a root beer at the Cone Zone. Still, her opinion matters. If she says something is sooooo cool, people listen to her. They have to. She's loud.

Gabby Jonas raised her hand.

"State your name," I said.

"Gabriella Carlotta Jonas the First!" she yelled.

4:43 p.m. "Do you have a question?" I asked.

"How do you know the future?"

"Trade secret," I said. I learned about those in *Mind Your Business* magazine. A trade secret means, "I don't have to tell you."

"I know the future, too," Gabby said mysteriously.

I took a deep breath so I wouldn't roll my eyes. Eye rolling is not acceptable professional behavior when you're trying to attract customers.

"Ooh!" said Susie Lorenzo. "What's the future, Gabby?"

"Peter's going to fall down!" Gabby announced. The six-and-under crowd cackled like it was the funniest thing they'd ever heard.

I cleared my throat to restore order.

"When do we get cupcakes?" asked Scott Mac-Gregor.

"Raise your hand!" Daniel yelled.

"No cupcakes yet," I said, making my voice

* 22 *

deeper. "I still have my Huge Announcement."

The crowd grumbled.

"Hey, show some respect!" Ken piped in. I nodded at him.

 BUSINESS TIP: Loyalty is the most important quality.

That goes for both employees and best friends.

Tom Reddi says you shouldn't mix business and friendship. Ken doesn't participate in my day-to-day operations, just special events. Still, he's an important member of my Inner Circle. He even loaned me his Version 5.7 Bionic Wireless Speaker for the launch party.

Tom Reddi says every leader should have an Inner Circle of people they trust. My Inner Circle is intimate. That means small and exclusive. It's only two people: me and Ken. When Granddad was alive, it was three.

"If we show some respect, *then* can we have cupcakes?" asked Scott.

"Yes," I said.

"I respect you," Scott said. "And cupcakes. I get the chocolate one on top. Chocolate is the best."

"No! Vanilla!" said Susie.

"Chocolate . . . chocolate . . ." Scott chanted.

"My favorite color is light green!" yelled Gabby.

My professional business launch was turning into amateur chaos.

 BUSINESS TIP: Cupcakes are great for drawing crowds but terrible for distractions. Weigh this decision carefully.

"All right," I said. I cleared my throat over and over until the noise died down. "My Huge Announcement is . . . I'm hiring an intern."

I waited for applause. Instead, Susie yelled, "Scott MacGregor gassed on my hand!"

I breathed deeply.

"Peter said he's hiring an intern!" yelled Daniel.

"What's an intern?" asked Scott.

"Raise your hand!" yelled Daniel.

Ken pulled out his limited edition Gulf Coast Gold EtherPhone 7. "An intern is . . . a political prisoner," he read. "Huh?"

I sighed. "*No.* An intern trains to become a business professional. The intern will be part of my prestigious Peter Presents, Inc., Internship Program."

BUSINESS TIP: Growth is essential. If you do what you've always done, you'll be who you've always been.

Hiring an intern is my Big Picture Goal for Q1. Interns work for you, but you don't have to pay them. It's a win-win situation. Now that Dad's out of work, I have to hire an employee so I can focus on generating income. That means making more money.

Mike the Unusual raised his hand. "How much does the intern get paid?"

"Interns don't get paid in money," I said. "They get paid in wisdom and experience."

The audience grumbled.

I wiped my face with my Peter Presents, Inc., Sweat Towel. Walking, talking, and amateur crowd management are too much for one person. Granddad gave me the towel after I made my first sale. "Don't let them see you sweat," he'd say.

"Moving on," I said calmly. "I'm going offline to read your essays." Going offline means "don't talk to me."

Ken walked over with the Crystal Ball of Opportunity.

"Guard the cupcakes," I told him.

"With my life," he said. That's loyalty.

I took the crystal ball to my Corner Office in the back of the garage.

———•———

Being a professional means having a professional workspace. I settled into my Executive Lawn Chair and read the first essay.

"S. A. That's my essay. (Get it? Say it out loud.)"

Clearly Scott MacGregor. Immediate disqualification.

Next.

"I want to work for you because I am a real superstar." Gabby Jonas. I rubbed my temples. First, she didn't even answer the question. Second, an intern is not a real superstar. Interns must be low status. Humble. It's part of the ecosystem.

Ecosystem. I learned that word from Tom Reddi. An ecosystem is a "community of organisms interacting with their environment." My cul-de-sac is an ecosystem. In an ecosystem, people have roles. There are amateurs and there are professionals. I'm a professional.

Ecosystem is also a science word. It's about the only thing I got right on my last earth science test.

The essays got worse. There were two more S.A. jokes and a drawing of a giant cupcake with clovers all over it.

Last essay. It started, "I know you're a very busy person and your time is valuable."

I raised an eyebrow. This person showed a real respect for the ecosystem.

This was my intern.

I made my way back to the stage where Daniel was break-dancing. He stopped when I held up my hand.

"We have a winner," I told the crowd.

I turned the paper over.

"Rachel," I said. "Rachel Chambers."

Peter Presents, Inc., Internship Application

(LIMIT ONE CUPCAKE PER APPLICANT)

NAME: Rachel Chambers

ESSAY TOPIC:
Why Do You Want to Work for Peter Gronkowski?

I know you're a very busy person and your time is valuable.

Hi. I'm Rachel. You're my neighbor, but we've never had a conversation. Is that weird? Maybe it's normal. A little about me: I was recently disqualified from a self-portrait contest. I'm pretty sure that's not normal.

I hope I don't get disqualified for saying this, but I'm not even sure I want a job. I just want to prove I'm not invisible. You'll probably pick Clover or Scott or some other loud person. I get it. But quiet people like me have a lot to offer, too.

I guess that's it. Thanks for the cupcake.

3

Rachel

"Rachel!" Clover yelled. "You won!"

"I won?" I said.

I'd never won anything in my life, except for Perfect Attendance. When they announced my name at the end-of-year assembly, everyone was talking over the principal.

"Rachel Chambers?" Scott MacGregor asked.

"Puppet!" said J. J. Roma, pointing a dirty fingernail in my face.

"Oh, yeah!" Scott said. "Nice one, Puppet!"

I gulped. Peter motioned for me to come onstage. Clover gave me a little shove. Then the crowd pushed me to the front of the room like a pinball.

Suddenly I was face-to-face with Peter Gronkowski. I'd never stood this close to him before. His turban was slightly crooked. He had zero freckles.

Peter wasn't an ordinary person. He was special. If he picked me to be his intern, he must have thought I was special, too. He believed in me and what I had to say.

I didn't just win. I was chosen.

"Congratulations . . ." Peter looked down at his card. "Rachel." His breath smelled like brownies. "You're the very first intern for Peter Presents, Inc."

Everyone stared like I was supposed to do something. What are you supposed to do when you win an intern essay contest? Take a bow?

I opened my mouth and waited for words to jump inside my brain. Clover gave me a thumbs-up.

"I can see you're too excited to speak," Peter said.

"This is going to be awesome!" Clover yelled. For a second I felt creaky, invisible puppet strings pulling my body.

But then everyone cheered. Not for Clover. For me.

My whole body felt warm, like I'd stepped out of my shell and into the sunshine.

"Excellent," Peter announced. "Cupcakes are served. Please show your wristbands."

Everyone cheered louder.

Peter turned to me and stuck out his hand. I shook it. His grip was firm and solid, while my hand flopped like a dying fish.

"Your internship starts tomorrow," Peter said. He handed me a green folder. "Just sign these Internship Guidelines to agree to the terms of employment. Welcome to Peter Presents, Inc."

Peter Presents, Inc., Internship Guidelines

Dear <u>RACHEL</u>,

Congratulations. If you're reading this, you've been selected for the exclusive internship program at Peter Presents, Inc.

Terms and Conditions:

1. You will not be paid in money. You'll be paid in business education and wisdom passed down by experienced entrepreneur Peter Gronkowski.

2. You must report to work by 7:55 a.m. However, please be on call 24–7 in case your services are required. That means all the time.

3. *BUSINESS TIP: Dress for the job you want.* You must wear proper business attire. IMPORTANT: If the attire is a costume, don't whine or complain about it. Your internship costume is:

ROBE, HEAD WRAP, GOLD JEWELRY

4. *BUSINESS TIP: No one is too good for hard work.*

Your duties will be:

WHATEVER I NEED YOU TO DO.

5. **IMPORTANT:** There's a zero-tolerance policy for lemonade at any Peter Presents, Inc., retail location.

Best,

Peter S. Gronkowski

Peter S. Gronkowski

Your signature:

Rachel Chambers

4

Rachel

That night, Clover and I searched through a trunk of my mom's old theater costumes. My fortune-teller intern uniform had to be perfect.

Clover grabbed a purple wig. "I looooo-oooooo-ve this!" she said. Clover has a lot of talents. One is that she can make any word about twenty syllables.

She wrinkled her nose at a navy blue suit. "This will *not* work," she said.

Here's a secret. Sometimes I put on that suit and pretend I won the Pulitzer Prize for *Cyrano's Revenge*. I practice my acceptance speech in the mirror: "I'd like to thank Dad, my dog Molly, Clover, and the original Cyrano, who sadly can't be with us today because he's dead." I could never give that speech in real life. I'd freeze into a block of ice, and the Pulitzer Prize people would push me offstage with a Zamboni.

"What's that?" Clover asked. She pulled out a black velvet drawstring bag I'd never seen before. Inside was a ring—a gleaming chunk of gold on a thin band.

I tried it on. It slid off my ring finger. On my thumb, it was a perfect fit.

Clover gasped. "That's the most beautiful ring I've ever seen in my life," she said.

I held the ring up to the light. It glittered like something magical.

It was Fate: winning the essay contest, the ring, all of it. Being an intern would be the best thing that ever happened to me. I'd be so confident I could sing "If I Were King of the Forest" backward and on my head for my Pulitzer Prize speech.

I was ready for anything.

———•———

After Clover left, I modeled my intern costume for Molly. She spun in a circle five times and wagged her tail. That's a good sign. When she doesn't like something, she plops flat on her side and sighs like you're disappointing her.

My intern costume felt like armor. I wasn't Puppet, or even Rachel Chambers. I was Fortuna (my secret intern nickname).

I took off the costume—most of it. I couldn't take off the ring. I mean, I could, but I just didn't want to.

The ring sparkled as I opened my *Cyrano's Revenge* notebook.

"Fate isn't always cruel," I wrote.

The ring even made my writing better.

"Rachel!" Dad called. "The evening meal is ready to commence!"

Dad can't just say that dinner is ready. He always makes it sound special, even though we usually have spaghetti.

I dropped my pen and ran downstairs. Dad was cracking noodles into a pot of boiling water.

"I brought you a new book," he said, nodding at the kitchen table. "Happy reading!"

It was *You Don't Say!: How to Speak Up*. Last week it was *Shy Guide: The Introverted Middle Schooler*.

"Thanks," I said. Ever since the "Rachel lives in a shell" parent-teacher conference, I have a feeling he's afraid I'm going to curl up in a ball and never uncurl.

Dad thinks every answer is in a book. But the

more books he brings home from work, the more I wonder if there's something actually wrong with me.

"My culinary assistant," Dad said. "Can you please bring me the salt?"

When I handed it over, his face turned kind of pale.

"Where'd you find that ring, Scoots?" Dad asked. Scoots is kind of a babyish nickname, but I like it. At least it's not Puppet.

"In Mom's old costume trunk," I said. "It's part of my fortune-telling intern costume."

"Ah," he said. He smiled a little. "I haven't seen that in years." He sprinkled salt in the boiling water. "That's Mom's engagement ring."

My eyes almost popped out of my head. "No way!"

"Scoot's Honor!" he said, holding up his right hand. He never gets tired of that joke. "All that glitters is not gold."

"Huh?" I asked. My dad is a quote factory, probably because he's a librarian surrounded by words all day. He's always saying random things and explaining them to me.

"The ring," he said. "Pretty good for a fake, right?"

"A fake?" I said. "You gave Mom a fake engagement ring? Isn't that . . . tacky?"

Dad laughed. "It's pyrite. Fool's gold. I told her I'd get her the biggest rock I could afford. And I did. She loved it."

My mom is more like a puzzle than a person. I collect stories about her and try to make a picture. There's always something missing, though. Dad doesn't really say much about her unless I ask, but I don't usually ask. It might make him sad.

"Sorry," I said. "I'll put it back."

"No, sweetie. Just be careful with it," Dad said. "Why hide it away? A thing of beauty is a joy forever."

I spun the ring around and tucked the warm stone in my palm. Maybe he was right.

After dinner, I went up to my room. I pulled out my favorite picture of Mom and me. We're in the laundry room. I'm three years old. She's folding a shirt and laughing, and I'm curled up in a laundry basket. She died one year after that.

In my head, she's laughing because I said something funny. I bet she knew about my secret joke talent even though I was only three.

I squinted close at her left hand in the picture. She was wearing the pyrite ring!

It was Fate, just like I wrote about in *Cyrano's*

Revenge. Mom wanted me to find her ring. It was a message saying she was on my side.

I put the picture down and looked in the mirror. Mom's beaded headband was on my bed behind me.

Before I could even think twice, I grabbed it and put it on fast.

I gasped. I didn't look like Mom. Just me, with some new accessories. I felt brave, like her.

"Fortuna, you are a leader," I told my reflection. I tried to raise an eyebrow, like Peter. It didn't work. I just looked like I had bad gas.

I pushed down on my left eyebrow and raised the right one. I did it five more times. My eyebrow muscle was stronger already.

Okay, so it didn't come easy for me like it did for Peter. I had to work harder.

CYRANO'S REVENGE

CHAPTER III

Cyrano, her sister, Tulip, and their loving parents were a family of common cow-milkers, as poor as poor could be. They lived in a barn made of sticks on the gloomiest hillside in Foggy Glen.

Tulip was Cyrano's most treasured friend as well as her sister. She was chatty and cheerful. Cyrano's words, on the other hand, were few but well chosen.

One day Cyrano wrote a poem and read it aloud to Tulip:

"Fate isn't always cruel.
My dearest family is a jewel
Of sun and sky,

Of golden rain.
Our love will pull us through again."

Tulip wiped a tear from her cheek. "Cyrano, I did not know these words were hidden inside your heart!"

Later, Cyrano read the poem to her parents around a fire of dying embers.

"You have a gift," said her father, who always knew exactly what to say. "There is strength behind your silence."

"Greatness is your destiny," said her proud mother, stroking Cyrano's hair. "You have important things to say."

"Mooooo," said the cows outside.

5
PETER

Ken stayed at my house after the launch party. He eats dinner with us on Fridays because his dad has a hospital shift and his stepmom meets with her adult-coloring-book group.

"This session of the Inner Circle Card Sharks will now come to order," I said.

"Can I shuffle?" Daniel asked.

I looked at Ken. He nodded.

"Request granted," I said.

Daniel whooped and threw the Go Fish cards all over the carpet.

Daniel's clearly not ready to be an official member of the Inner Circle. He's a Junior Associate. That means he plays on my team until he's ready for a promotion.

After Daniel picked up the cards, we started playing.

"The greatest monster movie ever is *Cannibal Cliff-Divers: On the Edge of Doom*," Ken said. "Go Fish."

While Ken was talking, Daniel tiptoed behind him.

I picked up a card. "No way," I said. "The greatest monster movie of all time is *RSVP: The Insane Invitation*. You screamed so loud you woke up Daniel."

"*Pssst! Peter!*" Daniel said in a loud whisper. He held up two fingers.

"Hey!" said Ken. He hugged his cards to his chest.

"Business tip: Insider information is illegal," I told Daniel. "Inner Circle Card Sharks must succeed through skill only. No cheating." But secretly I was proud of his loyalty. His promotion might be coming sooner rather than later.

"Okay, so *Insane Invitation* is the scariest," Ken said. "But not the *greatest*."

"Who's hungry?" Dad called. "I got Chinese take-out!"

"Baby corn!" Daniel yelled.

We put down our cards and went to the kitchen.

Right away I noticed something strange.

"Dad," I said. "Why is the Hog Wild jar empty?" The Hog Wild BBQ jar is where we keep all our spare change.

"Oh," Dad said. "They have this cool machine at the Reddi Mart. You put your change in and get it back in bills. The Hog Wild jar paid for tonight's dinner!"

He looked proud. Not embarrassed.

"Honey, takeout?" Mom said as she walked in from the garage. She set her briefcase on the uncracked end of the counter. Mom is a lawyer, but not the rich kind. She works for the government. "I thought we were watching our spending money."

 BUSINESS TIP: Don't talk about money in front of guests. Especially when your guests have more money than you do.

"You're right," Dad said. He kissed Mom and left a chocolate smudge on her cheek. "I lost track of time making Peter's cupcakes."

Sometimes I wonder if Dad is my real father. First, I don't bake. Second, I have a career. Dad is a stay-at-home dad (for now). Third, I never lose track of time. That's why I wear Granddad's watch. *Time is money.*

Granddad was definitely my grandfather. He owned a successful business called Gronkowski's Portable Garages. His associate, Frank T. Lillehammer, took over when he died. Now it's called Arnie's A-Plus Storage. There is no Arnie.

"Ken, let's get you something to drink," Dad said. He poured generic Cool Mountain Cola into old "Happy Birthday" paper cups.

I raised an eyebrow. "Cool Mountain Cola?" I said.

"Just try it," Dad replied.

 BUSINESS TIP: Brand names say luxury.

Before Dad got laid off, we drank real Coke. One day, when I'm a bona fide success, everything I own will have a brand name.

I took a sip. It burned my throat. "Gross," I said.

"It's gross?" Daniel asked. He took a sip and twisted his whole face. "Ew! It's so gross!"

"It's the same stuff as Coke, Peter," Dad said.

"No, it's not."

"Tastes the same to me," said Ken. He drank it all in one gulp.

 BUSINESS TIP: You can be nice or you can be honest. Choose wisely.

Tom Reddi says being nice is a sign of weakness. Leaders can't afford to be weak.

Dad folded a paper towel in his lap as we sat down to eat.

"How did the launch party go?" he asked me.

"Terrific," I said. "I hired my very first intern."

Mom raised an eyebrow.

Dad smiled. "When I was a kid, I had a lemonade stand," he said. "Ricky's Refreshments."

I cringed.

Lemonade stands don't make business sense. First, the market's flooded. Lemonade stands pop up in the cul-de-sac like dandelions. Dad says dandelions can be "useful." But I know dandelions are weeds. Weeds are meant to be destroyed.

Second, lemonade is a seasonal product. Nobody drinks lemonade in fall or winter. Some people here say it doesn't matter because it doesn't ever get that cold. Those people are amateurs. If customers buy lemonade in February, it means they feel sorry for you. Pity is not a sustainable business model.

Third, there's no barrier to entry. Any kid with a pitcher, drink mix, poster board, and markers can do it.

As long as I am the founder, CEO, COO, and CFO of Peter Presents, Inc., I will never sell lemonade.

7:04 p.m. Mom pushed some chicken around her plate with chopsticks. She doesn't eat much when she's getting ready for trial. "Peter, how's the King Midas project coming along?" she asked.

 BUSINESS TIP: Be vague, especially about school.

"Okay," I said.

That wasn't a lie. It was okay because I hadn't started it yet.

Every sixth grader at Poplar Middle has to give a presentation on a character from an ancient myth. I picked King Midas because Tom Reddi talked about him in the *Mind Your Business* "Midas Touch" issue.

I don't have time to read the King Midas story.

First, ancient myths are long. Second, I'm too busy stepping up as a breadwinner for this family. Here's the key takeaway: anything King Midas touched turned to gold.

 BUSINESS TIP: The "key takeaway" is the important lesson.

If King Midas were real, he would be my third mentor.

Tom Reddi says there's a lot to learn in the world, and most of it isn't in books. But when I tell Mom that, she gives me the Evil Eye. Speaking of books, *Mind Your Business* is the perfect size for hiding in books at school. Tom Reddi thinks of everything. I've never met him, but he makes things happen. The man is a bona fide success.

"What are you doing in school now, Ken?" Mom asked.

Ken and I don't go to the same school anymore. He goes to Poplar Prep. It costs $10,112 per year. Attending private school is a positive economic indicator. Using spare change to buy dinner is not.

Ken swallowed a mouthful of beef and broccoli. "Algebra," he said.

My heart beat faster. Poplar Prep isn't just a school. It's a fast track to success. The fast track goes: private school to Ivy League to B school. B school is business school, but no one who goes there calls it that.

Once we had to pick up Ken from school, so I got to go inside. Even the Poplar Prep air is different. It felt like coming home. The PP polo shirts. The branded PP backpacks. The PP prestige. PP even matches the initials of my business.

But my parents can't afford to send me there. That's why I have a Poplar Prep Savings Fund jar in my office. It has only seven dollars.

"What's on the Monster Movie Night agenda?" Dad asked.

Ken grinned. "*Attack of the Boring Blob*. A nerd blob gets revenge on the Bully Blob Squad by eating their faces off."

Daniel froze. A half-chewed piece of baby corn fell out of his mouth.

"It's not real," I told him. "It's from 1964."

"Sounds like a classic," Dad said. "I'll make us some popcorn. My new sweet-and-salty mix."

7:24 p.m. "I can't," I said. "Tomorrow is opening day. Businesses don't plan themselves."

"Aw, man," Ken said, looking down at his plate.

"We can still watch it," Dad told him.

"Okay," Ken said. He smiled. Every Friday Ken wants to watch Monster Movie Night on Scare TV. And every Friday he freaks out halfway through the movie. He covers his eyes and someone (me) has to tell him what's going on.

"Dad, don't you have other . . . plans?" I said. I didn't want to say "job searching" in front of Ken.

"Plans?" Dad asked. He shrugged. "Not really."

"I want fortune cookies," Daniel said. Noodles were stuck to his face, even his eyebrows. I could never take Daniel to a business meeting at Tom Reddi's Cone Zone with those table manners.

We cracked open our cookies and read our fortunes out loud. Mine was: "Be smart, be intelligent, and be informed." Ken's: "Reach out and touch the stars!" Mom's: "Humor is an affirmation of dignity." Dad's: "Why walk when you can soar?" Daniel's: "Jump! Someone will catch you." I read Daniel's for him since he can't read yet.

"Don't throw away your fortunes," I reminded everyone. "I need them for the business."

While Mom, Dad, and Ken cleaned the kitchen table, I took Daniel upstairs.

I helped him brush his teeth and reminded him to spit. After he changed into his monkey pajamas, we opened the latest *Mind Your Business*. He curled up close to me on the bed.

"We'll start with a 'Reddi Readers Talk Back' letter," I said.

Daniel sucked his thumb. His eyelids were already heavy.

"Dear Tom," I read aloud. "Big fan. Do you think great leaders like you are born, or can anyone learn to do it?"

I was only halfway through Tom's answer when Daniel started snoring. I hugged him and snuck out of the room.

Putting Daniel to bed reminds me what I'm working for: the future. Not just for me, but for my whole family.

I looked down. My shirt was covered in Daniel's drool.

 BUSINESS TIP: Drool is not professional.

7:46 p.m. Personal time was over. I changed into a fresh button-down shirt and tucked it in.

I headed downstairs to my Corner Office.

7:50 p.m. Made Business Activity Log.

7:52 p.m. Started list of Q1 Goals. Wrote "Hire an Intern" and "Make Business Activity Log." Crossed them out.

7:57 p.m. *Pop, pop, pop.* Smelled burning kernels and butter. They smelled generic.

8:19 p.m. Ignored Ken's shrieking.

8:23 p.m. Considered resale value of soy sauce packets and unused chopsticks. Outlook: Promising.

8:36 p.m. Wrote Mission Statement for Fabulous Fortunes: *Generate sufficient income to buy Chinese food to get more fortunes and pay parents' mortgage.*

8:41 p.m. Opened parents' mortgage statement from Poplar Bank.

8:42 p.m. Put "Gronkowski Mortgage Savings Fund" label on empty Mega-Mix Nuts jar and hid it under my desk, right beside my Poplar Prep Savings Fund.

8:44 p.m. Went upstairs for Success Snack: Little Buster's brownie and 2 percent milk. Heard Dad narrating the movie for Ken: "Now the nerd blob is—*oh!* Disgusting! There's a chunk of Bully Blob Number Three's nose on his snaggletooth!"

8:48 p.m. Read latest issue of *Mind Your Business*. Studied Tom Reddi's face on the cover. Imagined my face on the cover.

8:57 p.m. Flagged new article for Dad: "10 Tips for In-Your-Face Interviewing Success."

8:58 p.m. Wiped dust off laminated Peter Presents, Inc., calendar. In tomorrow's box, in black marker, wrote "First day of Fabulous Fortunes."

CYRANO'S REVENGE

CHAPTER XX

Years later, Cyrano's sister, Tulip, married Sir Michael the Strange.

Cyrano cried all through their wedding. How could her sister abandon her? What would Cyrano do? How would she survive on her own?

"Your time will come," her parents assured her.

"I care not about marriage," Cyrano said. "I only wish to forge my own path."

By day, Cyrano toiled on her parents' farm. By night, and by candlelight, she penned her poems. Over time, Cyrano earned enough money to explore life beyond cows. She applied to become an apprentice of the great poet Pouncey. Her application was accepted.

One chilly fall morning, Cyrano bid her parents a tearful farewell.

"Already my heart breaks from missing you," her mother said, sniffling into a handkerchief. "But you must follow your dreams."

"Stay just as you are, for you are enough," her father said, holding her close.

At sundown, Cyrano arrived at Pouncey's castle. It was tall, strong, and made of polished stone. Pouncey stood by the front gate with the air of a king.

"Cyrano!" Pouncey said. "Your application was bewitchingly beautiful, as are you. Your nose in particular is most pleasant. I feel a strong poetic connection between us." He touched his head, and then his heart. "Now let us begin our work."

6

Rachel

The next morning, I reported for duty by the Gronkowskis' front curb.

Peter was already there, leaning almost all the way back in a lawn chair. He had on the same outfit he'd worn at the launch party, but today he had a headset over his T-shirt turban.

"Hi—" I started.

Peter held up a finger and pointed to his headset. "I'll put you down for ten orders," he said into the mouthpiece. "Great doing business with you, Tom."

He clicked a button, then checked his watch.

"Terrific," Peter said. "You're on time. Business tip: Early is on time. On time is late."

"But . . . you said 7:55." Was this an intern riddle?

Peter didn't answer. He jumped up from the chair and started doing lunges. Right knee, left knee.

"Pregame warmup," he said.

I nodded like I understood what he was talking about. If I'd known the internship involved sports, I would've worn gym shoes instead of Clover's too-big gold flip-flops.

I twirled my ring and counted anthills in the sidewalk cracks.

"You've got to be hungry to have what it takes," Peter said between lunges. "Are you hungry?"

I nodded again, but I wasn't that hungry. I'd already had breakfast.

"Your first assignment," Peter said after his stretches. "Drape those sheets over the lawn chairs to make a tent."

As I draped, Peter stood off to the side. Every once in a while he said things like "Hm" and "That's crooked."

Then he took another business call. Who were these customers? How did you order fortunes by phone? It was very mysterious . . . and impressive.

I had so much to learn. Peter dripped knowledge like he sweat: a lot. So much that he kept wiping his face with a towel.

"Now," Peter said after I finished draping the tents. "Copy these fortunes in big letters." He handed me a pack of index cards, a marker, and crumpled slips of paper that smelled like soy sauce.

"Is there, um, a table I can write on?" I asked.

"Business tip," Peter said, tapping his watch. "Be resourceful."

The hardest surface I saw was the sidewalk, so I sat down.

The slips were fortunes from fortune cookies. I felt like I was cheating on a test as I copied them. Because the concrete was uneven, my letters came out all wavy.

"Ready for your most important duty?" Peter asked when I was done.

I sat up extra straight and nodded.

Peter took off his gold watch and handed it to me. "The official Peter Presents, Inc., timepiece is getting dingy," he said. "It needs to sparkle." He studied my face seriously, like he had given me a mission to save the world. "Can you handle this?"

"I . . . think so," I said. He handed me an old toothbrush and a cup of water.

"Here's the game plan," Peter said as I scrubbed imaginary stains. "The customer wears a blindfold. You'll hold up a fortune. I'll say it out loud. Got it?"

"Got it," I said.

Our first customer was Mel Chang.

"8:30 am. Right on time," Peter whispered. "Remember, Mel is a well-respected blogger. We have to impress her."

The first thing Mel said was, "Mel Chang, Poplar Lane blogger." I'm not sure why she said her name, since we already knew it. The second thing was, "What's new?" And before anyone could answer, she said, "Where are the refresh?"

Was that a complete sentence? I looked from Mel to Peter and back again.

"The refreshments," Peter said slowly. "Yes. My intern will take care of you."

I nodded confidently, like I refreshed and took care of people every day. As I walked next door to my house, I took extra-big steps like Peter. My steps were so huge that I got there really fast.

I checked the refrigerator for something, anything refreshing. There was a tall pitcher of water, but that wasn't refreshing enough. I added some ice from the freezer. Refreshing, but boring. I stirred in a few drops of green food coloring. Better. As a final touch, I added three baby carrots.

I carried the refreshments out on Dad's fancy silver serving tray.

"Would you like a glass of Truth Tonic?" I asked Mel.

Mel leaned into me, smelling like fake fruit and flowers. I leaned back. "Puppet?" she asked. "I didn't know you, like, had a voice."

"Truth Tonic?" I offered again, even though the last thing Mel needed was help in being honest.

She took a sip. "Yum," she said.

"Thanks," said Peter. "Old family recipe."

Old family recipe? Was that a joke? He didn't laugh. I didn't either.

"So, why carrots?" Mel asked me. She shoved her phone in my face.

"Why? Why. Why?" I repeated. My brain function froze. I suddenly wished Clover were there to pull my puppet strings.

I twirled my ring and channeled the spirit of Fortuna, Confident Intern. "Carrots," I said. "Carrots help you. They help you think. They have Vitamin A. It, uh, clears your head for fortune-telling."

Mel nodded, so I guess it sounded good. I had to admit, I was pretty proud of myself. It felt like writing a story, only I was saying the words out loud. I spoke, and someone listened.

Mel snapped a picture of the tray and tapped something into her phone.

We walked into the tent. Mel wrinkled her nose. "Disgust. Do I have to sit on dirt?"

Peter cleared his throat. "Pee waterfall," he mouthed. No, that wasn't it. Be . . . something. Recess pole? Then I remembered Peter's tip: *Be resourceful.*

"Just a second!" I said. I raced to my house and grabbed some pillows from the linen closet.

As I arranged the pillows for Mel, I hoped Dad wouldn't notice the grass stains.

"I need a few more pics for the blog," Mel said.

"My intern will set up the shoot," Peter said without looking at me. "Intern, position the Executive Lawn Chair."

I moved Peter's chair in front of the tent. Peter sat down, spread his legs wide open, folded his fingers in a "here's the church, here's the steeple" pose, and raised an eyebrow.

I stood off to the side while Mel snapped her photos.

When Mel was done, Peter pointed to a purple bandanna.

"Intern, tie the Blindfold of Destiny on Mel," Peter said. He settled back in his lawn chair and closed his eyes. I was the one who needed a nap.

I tied the bandanna around Mel's head, careful

not to crush her giant black glasses or tangle her super-long hair.

"Melllll," Peter bellowed in a low, mysterious singing voice. "We're here today to discuss your fuuuuuuture."

"Who's my homeroom teacher next year?" Mel asked.

"That's not how this wooooorks," Peter said. He was almost as good as Clover was at giving words a lot of syllables. "You don't ask queeeeeeestions. Your future is . . ." He motioned for me to hold up an index card. He squinted. "Don't look a gift horse in the mouth."

"What does that mean?" Mel asked.

"I don't offer transsssslations," Peter droned. "Noooooot part of my busssssssssiness model."

I waved one hand at Peter and tapped my head with the other. "I know," I mouthed. Peter raised an eyebrow. He made a scribbling motion with his hand. I grabbed a pen.

Peter wailed and moaned to fill the time while I wrote on a spare index card. "Hmmm . . . OOOOHHH . . . so very INNNNNNNTeresting . . . the future is so VERY BRIGHT . . ."

I held up my card, and Peter read it out loud:

"When you get a gift or something good happens, don't look for something to go wrrrrrrrrrrrrong. Appreciate it."

It's a good thing my dad is a quote factory. It comes in very handy for a fortune-telling internship.

Mel paused.

"That totes makes sense," she said. "I got a tiger tee from my Grandpa. And I haven't liked tigers since third grade. And I was going to sell it at the pawn shop. And now maybe I should keep it. Right?"

"Exaaaaaaactly!" Peter said. I already knew that business tip: the customer is always right.

I untied Mel's blindfold. She reached for her phone like it was water and she was dying of thirst.

"A few more Q's for the blog," Mel said. "Where do you get your fortunes?"

"What can I say? They just come to me," Peter said. "From the Great Beyond."

Huh? They came from Lucky Dragon Chinese Palace. It said so on the back of the fortunes.

I studied Peter's face. It didn't move. If I hadn't known the truth, I would've never guessed he was lying.

7
PETER

11:45 a.m. Sunday. Day 2 of Fabulous Fortunes.

Customer count: 3.

Amateur lemonade stand count: 3.

That's a 1:1 customer to lemonade-stand ratio. A solid B.

I settled into my Executive Lawn Chair and studied yesterday's data.

The first day of Fabulous Fortunes wasn't a total failure. Mel Chang, of course, gave me a five-star review. And I made thirteen dollars and fifty cents. Fortunes cost three dollars apiece, but Mel only paid one fifty for hers. She gets a half-price media discount.

 BUSINESS TIP: Prioritize your investments.

I put half my earnings in the Hog Wild BBQ fund (to finance more Chinese food and fortunes) and half in the Gronkowski Mortgage Fund. The Poplar Prep fund would have to wait.

Again, a solid B.

Mom would cry from happiness if I got Bs on my report card. But a B is an F in business. Tom Reddi says you can be in the black (that's good) or in the red (that's bad). My family was in the red. I had to do more.

Dad wasn't much help. He said he was "spending the weekend with his vegetables." Gardening is not a good economic indicator.

Tom Reddi says people who get laid off can get depressed. But hanging out with vegetables was more than depressing. It was like he didn't even care about finding another job.

"How's my watch?" I asked my intern through bites of Success Snack. "Is it sparkling?"

She held it up to the sun and nodded.

A woman of few words. An excellent quality in any intern.

Down the street, a huge machine drilled into the empty lot by Ken's house. It made the sidewalk shake.

Ken's house keeps getting bigger. The construction noise is very distracting for professionals like me who work mornings, afternoons, evenings, and weekends.

Ever since Dr. Spumoni got remarried, he's been spending a lot of money on home renovation. Mom says it's "sweet" because he's trying to impress his new wife. But Tom Reddi says marriage is not a wise business investment. He would know. He's been married three times.

11:47 a.m. Ken walked out of his house with two kids from Poplar Prep: Jose Benitez and Roderick Meyer the third. They always wore Poplar Prep polos, even on Sundays.

Jose and Roderick don't live in my cul-de-sac. They're from Fountain's Spout Landing, an up-and-coming development. Tom Reddi lives there, too. One day I'm going to be a Fountain's Spouter.

 BUSINESS TIP: Fake it till you make it.

"Give me my watch and headset, pronto," I told my intern.

I slipped them both on just as the guys walked up.

"Mr. Reddi!" I said into my headset. "Long time, no speak."

BUSINESS TIP: Wear a headset.

I paced around my lawn, taking huge steps. Movement attracts attention. Attention means people will see and hear you and know you're important.

"What's that?" I said. "I won the Promising Young Poplar Professionals Award? I'm honored."

 BUSINESS TIP: Make up awards. Give yourself trophies for them. Set the trophies out where people can see them.

I shook my head and laughed like he'd said something hilarious. "Hoo-hoo-ha. You're a wild man, Tom. See you on the range," I said. I pretended to hit a button to hang up.

 BUSINESS TIP: It's okay to pretend you're talking to someone.

"Gentlemen!" I said as Ken, Jose, and Roderick walked over. "Welcome to Fabulous Fortunes. Can I interest you in a peek into your future?"

"Hey, man," Ken said. "It's too noisy at my house. We're going on a Cone Zone run. Are you in?"

When Ken and I went to the same school, we did

Cone Zone runs all the time. We'd also go to the Reddi Mart for (real) Coke and beef jerky. I don't have that kind of time or disposable income anymore.

"No can do," I said. Jose and Roderick had on Vans. Real ones. My Dollar Palace loafers felt extra generic, even with my custom Peter Presents Logo. "I'm on the clock." I held up my hand so they could see my solid gold watch.

"No worries," Jose said. "You can meet us there on your lunch break."

No worries. Lunch breaks. Rich people don't get it. I work and go to school full-time. Lunch breaks don't exist.

"Today is a working lunch," I said.

"Can your assistant help?" asked Roderick.

"She's not my assistant," I said. "She's my intern." Then I had a brilliant idea.

"You know," I said, "she can hold down the fort for a while."

Here's why this was a brilliant idea. First, the guys would know I was more than just a successful one-man show—I was an empire. Second, it showed I could afford to take time off like a real rich person. The sign of someone successful is not working. It's making other people do the work.

Tom Reddi would call that "throwing money at the problem." But because interns work for free, I wouldn't spend a cent. That's a win-win situation.

My intern opened her mouth but didn't say anything.

"Be resourceful," I reminded her.

———————◦———————

 BUSINESS TIP: A true professional always buys the first round of drinks.

The total cost of four root beer floats at the Cone Zone is twelve dollars. I slammed fifteen dollars on the counter.

 BUSINESS TIP: You have to spend money to make money.

The money came straight from my Corporate Expense Account. I keep it in a special, hidden compartment of my wallet, not in a jar. An expense account shows people you have cash to burn.

"Keep the change," I told the waitress at the counter.

 BUSINESS TIP: Announce when you're leaving a tip. It shows high status.

Leaving a tip says, "You need this
more than I do."

We crowded into the corner booth. I call it the Power Booth because you can see everyone from there. That means they see you, too.

"Peter, do you like sports?" asked Roderick.

I snorted. It made bubbles in my float. "I don't have time for sports."

"Oh," said Roderick. "I like swimming."

"Me too, dude," said Jose. "We're getting a pool this summer. I'm gonna have a sick pool party. You guys are all invited!"

Ken and Roderick nodded. I nodded, too.

 BUSINESS TIP: Mirror the behavior of Important Relationships around you. They'll think you're just like them.

Even though I nodded, I knew I'd never see Jose's pool. Summer was my busy season.

Roderick burped. "That was awesome," he said. He had table manners like Daniel. "Now let's play some mini-golf!"

 BUSINESS TIP: Golf is a high-level executive duty. It forges connections.

Once *Mind Your Business* magazine did a cover story on the importance of golf. Tom Reddi said you could tell a lot about people by how they played. He also said to let your clients win.

I patted my pocket to make sure my wallet was still there. It was. But it was thin. I didn't have nearly enough funds for four tickets to Cone Zone Golf. Not paying would be an amateur move, though. A professional always pays for clients.

"Gentlemen," I said. "I'd love to show off my wicked slice." I didn't know what a wicked slice was. I just remembered it from the *Mind Your Business* golf article. "But I have to head back to the office. Responsibilities," I said. "You understand."

 BUSINESS TIP: Say "You understand" when you don't want to explain something.

They shrugged. They didn't understand.

"Hey, Peter," Ken said. "Wanna see the new Wave Crasher game?" He pointed across the room.

I checked my watch. "Two minutes," I said.

At the Wave Crasher game, Ken whispered, "Hey man, I've got you."

"You got me what?" I asked.

"If it's a money thing . . . I can pay."

"A money thing?"

My face burned. Ken and I never talked about money before. But now things were different. He had it, and I didn't.

"I don't need money," I said. "I have tons. It's just tied up in other investments right now."

"Oh, okay," Ken said.

I checked my watch. Time to end this conversation.

"Catch you later," I said.

Ken, Roderick, and Jose went up to the Cone Zone counter to pick out their clubs and balls. I walked home alone.

On the way back, I calculated the profit and loss of buying the root beer floats. The profit was making important business connections with pool owners. The loss was fifteen dollars.

My intern was sitting on the sidewalk when I got to my house. "How much money did you make?" I asked her.

"Twelve dollars," she said. She smiled like Daniel the first time he got all his pee in the toilet.

Twelve dollars. My chest felt a little less tight. That paid for the root beer floats before the tip. Deep down, I was impressed. Twelve dollars was not far off my all-time Peter Presents, Inc., single-morning record of thirteen dollars and ten cents (from Peter Presents, Inc.'s Mailbox-2-Doorstep Delivery Service, a one-day wonder. Brilliant but illegal, according to Mom).

"I'm disappointed," I said. "Our morning sales goal was twenty-one dollars."

 BUSINESS TIP: Tell employees you're disappointed in them. It motivates them to work harder.

My intern stopped smiling. She lowered her head and stared at the ground.

"I . . . I didn't know . . . there was a sales goal," she mumbled.

My intern's face crumpled.

I knew the signs of crying from being a big brother. First, a crumpled face. Second, a twisted-up mouth.

My intern's mouth twisted.

 BUSINESS TIP: Crying in the workplace is never, ever professional.

"Chin up," I said. "This is a learning experience.

Learn to be a better team player. Take it over the goal line. Blast it out of the park."

 BUSINESS TIP: Even if you don't have time for sports, use sports expressions. Using sports expressions says, "Business is a game and I am the winner."

My intern nodded. "I'm sorry."

I checked my watch. "Don't worry," I said. "You still have four hours to make up for it." I hated being such a softie. But I couldn't have crying in my workplace.

———•———

After the close of business, I met Dad in the garden.

"Are we having Chinese?" I asked hopefully. The Fabulous Fortunes fortune supply was running low.

"Smorgasbord," he said. He pushed a shovel into the dirt.

My stomach lurched. "Smorgasbord" means Dad finds whatever we have in the kitchen and makes something up for dinner. Smorgasbord is not a good economic indicator.

My Corporate Expense Account was empty. And

I had put all of today's earnings in the Gronkowski Mortgage Fund.

"We've got what we need here," Dad said. He smiled. "No takeout for a while, buddy."

No more Chinese food meant no more fortunes. And no more fortunes meant no more Fabulous Fortunes.

Wait. My intern wrote that terrific sentence about my being busy and important. That took talent. She could write my fortunes for free.

My shoulders relaxed. I was becoming a better boss by the second.

"These rocks are a drag," Dad said, plopping some in a bucket. He picked one out and tossed it to me. I caught it. "Want to hear something funny? Your aunt Sarah once had a pet rock."

"A pet . . . rock?" I sputtered. Aunt Sarah has signs in all her bathrooms that say, IF IT'S YELLOW, LET IT MELLOW. But a pet rock was goofy even for her.

"Seriously," Dad said. "People had pet rocks when she was a kid." Aunt Sarah is ten years older than him. *Mind Your Business* says large gaps between siblings is a wise financial decision. "Must be nice to be the guy that came up with that idea. He made millions of dollars."

I paused. "Millions?"

"Yup," Dad said.

The top of my head started to sweat. I tossed the rock back to him and ran inside.

I searched "pet rocks" on Mom's computer.

Dad was right. Pet rocks were a bona fide success. Gary Dahl, the guy who invented them, became a millionaire almost overnight. The rocks came with user manuals on how to take care of them and bonus products like a nest for your rock to sleep in. You could also draw faces on them and give them names and birthdays.

 BUSINESS TIP: A brilliant idea may seem terrible at first. But if something makes money, it is by definition not terrible.

I paced around the office. My head dripped like I'd eaten five Reddi Mart spicy burritos in a row.

The New Biz Buzz. It happens every time I get a brilliant business idea.

I sat down in Mom's chair to Visualize. I fluttered my eyelids and imagined two business advisors, one on each of my shoulders.

"It's too soon to try something new," the left-shoulder advisor said. "Fabulous Fortunes is a bona fide success. Don't spread yourself too thin. You're doing great things for women in the workplace by hiring a female intern. Your empire is on track."

"If I may," the right-shoulder advisor cut in. "Rocks are a sure thing. They're everywhere. Zero up-front costs. All you have to worry about is labor—digging them out of the ground. You wouldn't do that, of course. That's what interns are for." He turned to the left-shoulder advisor. "You understand."

The left shoulder advisor vanished into thin air.

I sprinted to the library. Mr. Chambers was locking the front doors when I got there.

"Mr. Chambers?" I said, trying not to pant. "I need some books on rocks. It's an emergency."

"Ah, Peter," he said. "A day's work is never done."

"That's a good one," I said.

He sighed and waved me inside.

Walking home was tough because rock books are heavy. But the New Biz Buzz kept me going. I saw a future, and it was in rocks.

 BUSINESS TIP: Good ideas can come from anywhere.

Even from amateurs like Dad.

8

Rachel

"Be resourceful," Peter said as he walked off to the Cone Zone with his friends. I was all alone.

I felt as helpless as the baby squirrel Dad and I found in Poplar Park last year. He had fallen out of a tree. We called Poplar Squirrel Rescue, and they saved his life.

There was no Poplar Rachel Rescue. I was adrift in a sea of lemonade stands.

"Hi, Puppet," said a voice behind me.

I spun around to find Susie Lorenzo.

"I need a fortune," Susie said, twisting her hands like it was the middle of class and she had to pee.

"Sorry," I said. "The Amazing Peter is, um, on a retreat. He's not here right now."

Susie's bright blue eyes filled with tears.

"But I need a fortune now," she whispered. "Can you tell me a fortune?"

"I—" I started to say no. But if Peter heard there was a crying customer at his business, I'd be in serious trouble.

"Okay," I said. "Please take a seat in the Pillow Palace."

Susie went into the tent. I pawed through the Mobile Workplace wagon, searching for the fortunes.

"Oh no," I said out loud. Peter kept the extra fortunes in his wallet.

"What?" called Susie from the tent.

"Nothing!" I called back.

I did ten jumping jacks and five lunges.

"You've got this, Fortuna," I whispered. How hard could fortune-telling be? I was a writer. It was like telling a story, but out loud.

I twirled Mom's ring around my thumb. When I touched the pyrite, I felt a shock that was almost electric.

I stepped inside the tent.

"Close your eyes, Susie," I said in a low and mysterious voice. "I am Fortuna. Let my spirit wash over you."

"Okay," said Susie. She closed her eyes.

"Now," I said. "What do you want to know?"

"What will I be when I'm fifty-six?"

"Um," I said. "Um." That was a lot of pressure for my first independent fortune.

If this were one of Peter's fortunes, it would say something like, "May the wind be in your sails." But Fortuna could do better than that. And Susie deserved more for three dollars.

I eyed Susie's striped leggings, YOU'RE BACON ME HUNGRY T-shirt, and blonde side braid with rainbow ribbons on the ends.

"You will be . . . a fashion designer," I said.

Susie opened her eyes. She broke into a huge grin. "That's so good!" she said.

My heart swelled with pride. I pictured Susie taking a bow at the end of a runway, the most successful fifty-six-year-old designer in fashion history.

Susie pulled out her money. "That's a really designive dress, Fortuna," she said. "I'm very interested of that color purple." Susie kind of talks in her own language. I call it Susie Speak. She doesn't always get the words right, but you know exactly what she means.

"Thanks," I said.

"I'm gonna tell all my friends to come see you to-day!" she said as she ran off.

Susie kept her word. And I, Fortuna, predicted the futures of three more Poplar Elementary students, on the spot, all by myself.

Being an intern might sound glamorous, but it was way harder than it looked. My back ached from all the fortune-telling. I crouched down on my regular spot on the sidewalk. Out of the corner of my eye I saw Peter's lawn chair. It was very padded, and very empty.

I checked to make sure no one was watching. In this cul-de-sac, someone was usually watching. Then I got up and sank into the oversized seat.

"Ahhhh," I said. For the first time that day, my tired muscles relaxed.

Peter's headset was propped up against the chair. I slipped it on. It was too big for my head, but it felt just right.

———◦———

And what did Peter say when he got back?

"I'm disappointed."

His words hit me like a dodgeball to the teeth.

I almost, almost cried. If crying were falling off

a cliff, I would have been hanging on with my left pinky toenail.

It's not like I almost cried because I was sad or ashamed. I wasn't. It's that I wanted to say so many things, like how many customers came in. How many fortunes I'd made up, on the spot. How absolutely, 100 percent positive I was that there was no morning sales goal. But I couldn't make myself say anything. That made me almost as mad at myself as I was at Peter.

Almost.

Later that afternoon, Peter slipped on his headset. "Terrific, Tom," he said into the mouthpiece. "I'll put you down for ten orders."

Who was Tom? Why did he keep calling? Why didn't the phone ring? Why did he always want ten orders? How could Peter hear the other person talk when his earpiece was on the outside of his head wrap?

Maybe Tom wasn't even real. Maybe he was as phony as Peter's fortunes.

Peter folded his hands behind his head and spread his legs wide like he was saving seats on the bus. "Hoo-hoo-ha!" Peter said. It was the fakest laugh I'd ever heard. "Tell the wife I said hello."

He pressed a button to hang up. He stared into the distance with an amazed look on his face, like he'd just seen a comet in broad daylight.

"Intern," he said. "Bring me my pen and note-book."

Intern. As I gathered Peter's supplies, the word echoed in my head. He never, ever called me by my name. It was, "Intern, do this," or "My intern will do that." *My.* I didn't belong to him.

Peter thought he owned everything, including me. He was like a dog that never stopped marking his territory.

I knew what he thought. He thought I was some dumb amateur who didn't understand anything about business. But I'd made twelve dollars today.

And none of it was mine.

CYRANO'S REVENGE

CHAPTER XXII

Pouncey the poet was not as he seemed. He did not teach; he did not write. He only marveled at his reflection in the castle's moat while poor Cyrano looked after the pigs.

When Pouncey addressed Cyrano (a rare event indeed), he spoke in hollow riddles disguised as wisdom.

"Poet's creed," he'd say. "The sky is blue, and water, too."

Cyrano began to wonder if they had any poetic connection at all.

One morning Cyrano woke to find her poems gone. She approached Pouncey in a panic.

"The pigs ate my poems while I slept!" Cyrano said. "Might I move from the pigpen into your servants' quarters?"

Pouncey laughed. "Hoo-hoo-ha. You wish to sleep in my castle?"

Cyrano looked up at his five-hundred-room monstrosity. "I do not take up much space."

Pouncey glared. "You make me late for my poetry reading, apprentice. I cannot keep my fans waiting. Poet's creed: Apprentices stay in the shed." He stormed off.

"That's not a poem!" Cyrano shouted after him. Angrily she donned her cloak and followed Pouncey through the darkness.

———•———

"Fate isn't always cruel," Pouncey recited to his adoring audience. "My dearest family is a jewel . . ."

Cyrano gasped. Those words were hers. Pouncey, not the pigs, had stolen her poetry!

Cyrano felt deep sorrow for having accused her pink, snorting companions. The real and true pig was Pouncey. Nay! Pigs are gracious and kind. Pouncey was not fit to eat their slop. Pouncey was a subpig.

9

Rachel

I chewed my pen. The hardest part about being a writer is doing mean things to your characters.

I didn't want Pouncey the poet to betray Cyrano. But he had to, otherwise she wouldn't get revenge, and my book is called *Cyrano's Revenge* for a reason.

Cyrano has secret royal blood and will become queen of the world. *I* know that because I'm writing it. But Cyrano doesn't know that yet. She only knows how it feels when someone treats you like you don't matter. And everyone wants to matter, even if they don't say it out loud.

Like me.

But nobody was writing *my* story. And I was pretty sure I wasn't secret royalty.

I ran downstairs and read Mel Chang's five-star

review for the hundredth time: "A Man. An Empire. Peter Presents: Fabulous Fortunes." My name wasn't mentioned once, not even as Puppet or Fortuna. It was like I didn't even exist.

I should have been proud of that review. After all, I was part of the Peter Presents team. I'd earned at least two and a half of those stars. But I didn't feel like a player. I felt like the person on the sidelines who squeezes water into the real players' mouths.

Dad says respect is a two-way street. Peter would want me to stand up for myself, right? That would show him I was an equal, not a barnacle.

I needed help from a real professional, so I went to Google. I searched "How to talk to your boss."

It turns out a *lot* of people don't like their bosses. I scanned the first post on a blog called "Intern No More: Get Your Own Coffee (Angry Annie's Story)." Angry Annie typed in all capital letters:

"PROVE URSELF!" she said. "SHOW UR BOSS WHAT UR WORTH!"

I don't really know what I'm worth. But I know I'm worth something.

I'd give Angry Annie a C for spelling, but she had a point.

———◆———

All week long, I practiced what to say to Peter. By Saturday, I was ready. Terrified, but ready.

It was 7:53 when I walked outside. That seemed either early or on time enough for him not to complain.

Peter was leaning almost all the way back in his lawn chair, holding a book over his face.

I cleared my throat. "Ahem," I said. Peter didn't move. "AHEM!"

Peter looked up from *A Rockhound's Guide to Limestone*. "Are you sick?" Peter asked. "You can't be sick. Interns don't get sick days."

"I'm not sick." *But thanks for your concern*, I thought.

"Good," Peter said. "Business tip: Sickness in the workplace damages productivity." He pulled the lever on his chair, sat up, and scribbled in his notebook.

"Can I talk to you?" I asked.

"We're talking now," he said.

Why did Peter have to make every interaction complete torture? "I know. I want to talk to you about . . . something."

He checked his watch. "You have five minutes."

I breathed through my nose. That's supposed to calm you down. But I still felt like a jumping bean. I spun my ring around my finger. That helped, a little.

"I want, um." I cleared my throat. "I want to be paid."

Peter's face didn't move, not even an eyebrow twitch. He was still and quiet . . . slow-motion quiet, the kind that stretches on forever.

"Paid?" he said. "You signed a contract. Interns aren't paid. You knew that."

"Yeah," I said. "But I've done a lot for Fabulous Fortunes." I pulled a list out of my robe pocket. "I increased sales by thirty-five percent. I created original ideas like Truth Tonic and the Pillow Palace. I translated fortunes for you. I even made up fortunes by myself. And I, um, add value to your watch by cleaning it."

Peter set his elbows on the lawn chair armrests and folded his fingers into a tent. "Frankly," he said, "I'm concerned."

"Concerned?"

"I'm concerned that you see your internship as a challenge and not an opportunity."

"What opportunity?" I asked.

"An opportunity for growth. An opportunity to make a difference." Peter sounded like he was reading a brochure from the guidance counselor. "Interns are amateurs. I can't pay an amateur. It's not professional. You understand."

"No," I said. "I don't understand."

Peter's stone face shifted. "You don't understand?" he said.

"No," I said. I couldn't believe that word came out of my mouth. *Twice.* I almost did feel like a puppet, but this time I was pulling the strings.

"No?" said Peter. "Huh-huh-huh." This laugh sounded different from his phone laugh. It was real. And mean. "You know how I know you're an amateur? Because a professional would never talk to their boss like this. You're walking a fine line."

I was. I could feel it.

Peter stood up and patted me on the back. I felt his icy alien touch through my fleece bathrobe.

"You'll get there," Peter said. "Someday." He snapped his fingers. "Wait. I have a brilliant idea. Your new and improved title is *head* intern."

"Um . . . okay," I said. Head intern? I was the only intern.

"And there's more!" Peter said. He sounded like a game show host. "I'll give you another title: Head Fortune Writer. You're in charge of writing *all* the fortunes from now on. No more copying fortune cookies. Exciting, right? This is your chance to shine. To show the world your unique voice."

I searched Peter's face. He was serious. He really thought making me do more work for free was some kind of reward.

"And!" Peter announced. His pupils were almost spinning, like being generous was hypnotizing him. "I'll give you a free fortune." He held up a hand. "I won't take no for an answer. Your money is no good here."

Peter gave me an index card from the wagon. In my wobbly sidewalk-handwriting, the card said: "Don't get mad: Get even."

I opened my mouth. Nothing came out.

I folded the card into a thousand tiny squares and shoved it in my bathrobe pocket.

Peter checked his watch. "Your five minutes are up. Really terrific chat. Oh," he said, taking off his watch, "this is getting dingy again. Can you be extra careful scrubbing it this time? I need you to do better."

He picked up his book and leaned way, way back in his lawn chair, almost horizontal to the ground.

A secret, mean part of me wanted to tip him over. Watch him fall.

I gripped the watch tight. Last week's spelling test word flashed in my brain: *arrogance*. It means you think you're better than everyone else. Did arrogance mean you thought you were too good for gravity, too?

I crouched down on my regular spot on the sidewalk. When I knew Peter couldn't see me, I spit on the watch. I rubbed in my spit with the toothbrush. It shined brighter than ever.

"All done," I said.

10
PETER

4:37 p.m., Friday. Dad said we were having Smorgasbord for dinner. Again.

I called Ken to cancel Monster Movie Night.

"Oh," he said. He sounded disappointed. "Can we still play cards?"

"Sorry," I said. "No can do."

First, I had too much work. Launching a groundbreaking business while you're already running one is hard. Second, playing cards is personal, not professional. Third, I didn't want Ken to know we were eating Smorgasbord for dinner. Nobody at Poplar Prep had to eat Smorgasbord.

———•———

5:09 p.m., Saturday. I was printing ads for my new operation when Mom stormed into the office. She slammed a piece of paper down on the desk.

"What is this?" she demanded.

It was a report card. It was mine. And it wasn't good.

I try not to argue with Mom because she's a lawyer. She argues for money. That means she's good at it. Our house is like a courtroom, and she's the prosecution, judge, and the jury. No chance for a fair trial, if you ask me.

"That's a report card," I said.

 BUSINESS TIP: Maintain a calm, even voice during confrontation.

Mom's green eyes flashed like numbers on the New York Stock Exchange ticker. "Don't get smart, Peter." She picked a page off the warm printer. "'Peter Presents: Rocks Rock!'? No, sir. You are not starting yet another business with a D in social studies. You failed the state capitals test."

Little hairs I didn't know I had stood up on the back of my neck. Mom had been mad before, but she'd never threatened to take away my heart and soul: business. And it wasn't just *my* business. Our family needed my help.

Everyone was focused on the wrong thing. Failing social studies? Please. State capitals have zero importance in my life. The *other* kind of capital— money—that's what mattered.

Still, Mom had high status in the household. She liked to say, "You may be the businessman, but I'm the boss." Sometimes I wonder if she reads *Mind Your Business* when I'm not looking.

"And what about your King Midas project? Your presentation outline was due last week," she said. "Mrs. Hargreaves told me you haven't even read the story yet!"

"I read the first part," I said. I folded my hands into a Power Tent. "I'm really looking forward to reading the rest."

Mom's Evil Eye didn't blink. Time to negotiate. "I promise to study one extra hour after dinner every night," I said.

Mom raised an eyebrow. "Not good enough." She stared me down. "Your father and I are also concerned that you're not spending enough time with the family."

Interesting move. A surprise witness: "your father."

While we were on the subject, I was "concerned" that Dad was spending too much time with plants and not enough time with his résumé. But could I tell Mom that? No. I'd get grounded. I'd never run a business again. We would be homeless. Worst of all, they'd cancel my subscription to *Mind Your Business*.

So I introduced my own surprise. "I agree, Mom," I said.

 BUSINESS TIP: Agreement *always* **throws people off. Especially parents.**

Mom raised the other eyebrow. "Really?"

"Yeah," I said. "I miss spending time with you guys." That wasn't 100 percent true. I like my family, but I live with them. How can you miss people you live with?

Daniel burst into Mom's office, almost knocking over the desk lamp. "Can I play business with you, Peter?" he asked.

Little kids can say dumb stuff, but at that moment, Daniel was the smartest human being in the world.

I threw an arm around his shoulder. "Sure, Danny Boy. Hey, how'd you like to be my next intern? Then we can spend more time together." I paused, meeting my mom's glare. "As a family."

"Yay!" Daniel hugged my knees.

Mom is tough, but she's not a diamond (the strongest rock in the world).

"We'll see," she said. "We'll see" means "I'm gonna make you sweat." It wasn't a done deal. But her eyes got soft around the corners. That's her "tell." A tell is a sign of weakness. Tom Reddi says everyone has one.

"I want to play business *now!*" Daniel whined.

Inside I groaned, but I plastered on a big grin. "Sure, Danny Boy!"

I dragged Daniel into the backyard.

"What do I do, Peter?" he asked. He was like a puppy nipping at my heels—a puppy in Dollar Palace light-up sneaker skates.

Mom stood by the kitchen window, watching us.

"Dig," I ordered, handing him a shovel. "Pull out whatever rocks you can find. Put them in the bucket. And laugh. Make it look like you're having fun."

"Fun!" Daniel yelled.

"Hoo-hoo-ha," I said, patting him on the back. Mom sipped her coffee and walked away from the window. Score.

At Smorgasbord dinner, Dad said, "I hear you're expanding the family business! Gronkowski Brothers, together at last."

I folded my paper-towel napkin in my lap. "I'm not changing the name," I said. "It will always be Peter Presents, Inc."

"Rick, I'm worried they'll destroy your beautiful garden," Mom said.

"That's okay," Dad replied. "I have to reseed most of it later this spring anyway. This'll be fun!"

Mom rubbed her temples. "Okay."

Dad winked at me.

I hate when Dad calls my work "fun." Would he go into Mom's law office and wink at her and ask how much fun she's having? No. Work is fun, to me. But when other people say "fun," they mean "play."

My new intern shoved spaghetti strands up his nostrils.

I fluttered my eyelids and Visualized. I needed to reframe this challenge as an opportunity. At least Daniel would never ask for money like my current intern. That is, my soon-to-be-former intern.

 BUSINESS TIP: Like 2 percent milk, employees have an expiration date. Firing them is business. It's not personal.

To: secretchambers@poplarmail.com
From: CEOutstanding@peterpresents.com
Re: Cardboard box

Dear Intern,
Assignment: Bring a cardboard box to work
tomorrow.

Best,
Peter (Your Boss)

* * *

Peter Gronkowski
Founder. CEO. CFO. COO. Entrepreneur. Innovator.
Empire.
PETER PRESENTS, INC.

11

Rachel

I read Peter's email five times. A cardboard box? What new intern duty did I have now? Building a display case for his trophies?

I turned off the computer and went up to my room. It didn't matter. I was going to quit anyway. Tomorrow would be my last day as an unpaid intern, forever and always.

That night I wrote a quitting speech. I guess being Clover's speechwriter helped. I put on the suit from Mom's costume trunk to pump myself up.

Then I practiced with Molly.

"This isn't a good fit for me," I told her. "Thank you for the opportunity." Molly spun in five circles and wagged her tail, so I knew it was really good. I wished I could wear the suit for my real speech tomorrow, but Peter was strict about the dress code. As much as I hated it, he was still my boss for one more day.

My speech was a lot nicer than the things I wanted to say. But Dad says you shouldn't burn bridges. That means you shouldn't end things badly, even if you're mad. That's especially true when your boss is your neighbor, since you still have to see him all the time.

———◇———

The next morning, I got to work so early there was fog on the windows when I left my house. Peter was already outside, sitting in his lawn chair. He wore a dark blue suit. His hair was gelled and parted so straight I could see his scalp.

I shivered, and not just because it was chilly. A suit? Where was his costume?

Daniel sat on the ground beside Peter, scrubbing his gold watch with a toothbrush.

My heart jumped around like it was trying to get my attention. *Hey, you!* it said. *Yeah, you! Run!*

I stood like I was planted to the ground.

"Have a seat," Peter said. He gestured to the

grass, staying seated in his chair. What a gentleman.

"Hi, Puppet!" Daniel waved at me with the toothbrush.

"I want to thank you for your service," Peter said.

Seriously, I'm talking to you! my heart said. *Leave! Now!*

Peter nodded at Daniel. Daniel stared at Peter. Peter cleared his throat and gestured to the wagon.

"Oh!" said Daniel. He walked to the wagon and brought me a folded sheet of paper.

"This was a difficult decision," Peter said. "But I'm afraid I have to let you go."

"Let me go where?" I asked. The top of the paper said LETTER OF TERMINATION.

Termination. Terminate means "stop." The end.

I dropped my cardboard box.

"I'm fired," I said. "You're firing me."

"It's more of a layoff," Peter said. "I'm sunsetting Fabulous Fortunes. Moving on to a new and exciting opportunity. You understand."

"But . . . but . . . I was going to quit!" I sputtered. "I have a quitting speech! I even wrote it down!" I pulled the paper from my pocket. A gust of cold wind blew it out of my hand, and it tumbled off down the street. Daniel ran to chase it, but Peter held up his hand.

"When people are *let go*," Peter said, talking slowly like he was training a monkey, "they say things they *don't mean*."

His fingers wiggled on the armrests of his lawn chair. I bet he couldn't wait to write down how brilliant he was in his obnoxious notebook.

Another gust of wind came, blowing my skirt around. I was done, finished, all because Peter Gronkowski said so. He was in a suit, and I was in a bathrobe.

He stood up. "Don't worry. I won't hold it against you. Please gather your things. They should fit in your cardboard box."

The red wagon was piled high with junk. Almost everything had a sticker that said PROPERTY OF PETER PRESENTS, INC. I grabbed Dad's Truth Tonic pitcher, his fancy silver tray, and our pillows. Everything looked blurry and wet, like Clover's famous watercolor cat sculpture.

Oh no.

No, no, no. *Do not cry*, I told myself.

Hot tears spilled down my face. My own body didn't even listen to me.

"Business tip," Peter said. "Crying in the workplace is not professional. That tip will help you at your next internship."

I wiped my tears with my fist. *There will never, ever be another internship.*

"You'll have to be escorted home by security," Peter said. "Standard procedure. Daniel?"

"I didn't steal anything," I said through gritted teeth. *Unlike you*, I wanted to add. *You steal ideas, you steal credit, you steal time. And you don't even care.*

Then I realized something even more awful. Every kid in the cul-de-sac was watching my termination. Their faces were pressed up against foggy glass windows. Clover, Mike the Unusual, Ken, Mel Chang . . . all witnesses to my humiliation. I hung my head low, like not seeing them would make them disappear. But when you live in a circle, there's no escape.

Daniel grabbed my bathrobe sleeve.

"Okay, Puppet!" he said. "You're coming with me."

"Daniel," Peter said. "When you get back, please clean up the workspace. That's your next duty as my new official intern." He walked back to his house, taking gigantic steps. He didn't look back.

New intern. I'd been replaced by a four-year-old.

"Sorry, Puppet," Daniel said when we reached my doorstep.

"It's Rachel," I said, but not in a mean way. I felt sorry for him, too. His brother was an evil dictator.

I ran up to my room, ripped off my intern costume, and threw it against the wall. Molly whimpered and hid under my bed.

Luckily, Dad was at work so I didn't have to talk to anybody. I curled up under my covers. The phone rang, and then the doorbell. I was sure it was Clover, but I couldn't face anyone, even her.

———◦———

I must have cried myself to sleep, because the next thing I heard was Dad yelling: "Prepare for a Far East feast. We're having Chinese!"

As if the day couldn't get any worse.

I walked into the kitchen like a zombie. My body ached from crying.

"Your eyes are red, Scoots," Dad said. "Is something the matter?"

"Allergies," I lied.

Dad talked all through dinner, mostly about library stuff. I focused on my chopsticks. They seemed like good weapons.

"What did those water chestnuts ever do to you?" Dad asked.

"Huh?" I looked down. They had holes. I guess I was poking them pretty hard.

After dinner, Dad asked, "Care to partake in a fortune cookie?"

"No!" I yelled. Just the thought of fortune cookies made me want to puke. Their lemony-fake cookie smell, the fake fortunes inside . . . everything about their fakeness reminded me of Peter. "Fortunes are a *lie*."

"Whoa, Nellie," Dad said, holding up his hands.

He read his fortune out loud, and I hummed to myself in my head so I wouldn't hear it.

We cleaned up the kitchen after dinner.

"What are these?" I asked, pointing to a pile of books on the island. *The Rock Chronicles. Be a Backyard Rockhound. Excellent to Extraordinary!*

"Ah, for Peter," Dad said. "Seems he's been bitten by the bookworm. He asked me to bring them home. Would you mind running them next door to-morrow?"

My own father, a traitor. Even he was under Peter Gronkowski's evil spell.

"Would I mind?" I said. It felt like I was spitting words. "Would I *mind*? Yes! I would mind! I'm not your unpaid intern!"

"Scoots," Dad said. His eyes darted around, like he was trying to find words and put them in the right order. "Are you okay? You can talk to me. I'm on your side."

"*I'm on Your Side* is the name of one of your dumb books!" I yelled. "I saw it in the bathroom! And *no*, I'm not okay!"

Dad didn't look mad. More like scared. That's how I felt, too. I'd never talked to him, to anyone, like that in my whole life.

I didn't think I had tears left, but I guess I did. I cried and cried some more. Dad held me close. When I could finally breathe, I told him everything.

Dad smoothed a frizzy piece of hair on top of my head. "When one door closes, another one opens," he said.

"What does that mean?"

"The end of something can mean the beginning of something even greater."

I thought about doors opening and closing. I pictured slamming one shut on Peter Gronkowski's face, but I don't think that's what Dad meant.

Later Molly followed me up to my room.

"I'm sorry for scaring you," I told her. "I won't throw an intern costume ever again."

She didn't seem to hear me. She pawed at the window.

"What's wrong?" I asked her.

I peeked outside and found Peter and Daniel digging in their backyard. Well, Daniel was. As usual, someone else was doing Peter's dirty work.

Work.

Something in my brain clicked like a locker combination.

1. Peter (Daniel) was digging in his backyard.
2. Peter asked Dad to bring home rock books from the library.
3. Peter said he was "moving on to a new and exciting opportunity."
4. Peter would think rocks from his backyard were new and exciting.

Conclusion: Peter was selling . . . rocks?

Peter was selling rocks! Only Peter Gronkowski would try to sell something you could get for free.

"*Aha!*" I said to Molly. I put up my hand so she would give me a high five. She cocked her head.

"We'll work on that later," I said.

I jumped up and started pacing. I had no clue what to do with this top secret information or my new, frantic energy.

I put on fresh pajamas and straightened up my room. Before I threw my Fortuna bathrobe into the laundry basket, I checked the pockets. There was a folded index card in one of them. It was my fortune, the one Peter gave me, in my wavy handwriting: *Don't get mad—get even.*

NOTICE OF SILENT PERIOD

Dear Poplar Lane,

Thank you for supporting my extremely successful business: Fabulous Fortunes. It's been a pleasure fortune-telling just for you. I've learned so much about your hopes, dreams, and desired homeroom teachers.

As my mentor Tom Reddi once said, part of being great at business is knowing when to move on. So I've decided to sunset Fabulous Fortunes. That means I'm not doing it anymore.

Don't worry. I'm not gone for good. I'm taking a silent period of five business days as I work on my next big project. It's going to *ROCK*.

Geologically yours,

Peter S. Gronkowski

Founder, CEO, CFO, and COO of Peter Presents, Inc.

P.S. There will not be a corporate launch party. The last one was an amateur disaster.

P.P.S. Peter proudly welcomes Daniel Gronkowski to the Peter Presents, Inc., family. Daniel will be Peter's intern and right-hand man. Daniel comes to the job with a positive attitude and 4.5 years of life experience.

12

Rachel

Don't get mad, get even.

The fortune in my bathrobe pocket felt like destiny. The best way to get even with Peter Gronkowski was to be his competition.

I set the fortune on my nightstand, right beside my open *Cyrano's Revenge* notebook. I always wrote before bed. It's when my brain could finally focus.

But I shoved the notebook in the drawer and slammed it shut. Writing *Cyrano's Revenge* would have to wait. I had real revenge to worry about.

I ran downstairs to Dad's office and turned on his computer.

In the browser, I typed "starting a business." Only one billion four hundred forty million hits.

I scrolled down the page and clicked the thirteenth link. *Lucky number thirteen*, I thought.

Random images filled the screen: a lightbulb, an equal sign with a slash through it, a magnifying glass, and a question mark. Huh? Before I knew what was happening, an envelope appeared, flashing a message:

"WARNING! URGENT! TIME-SENSITIVE NOTICE INSIDE! CLICK TO OPEN NOW!" A countdown clock beeped down the seconds: "20 . . . 19 . . . 18 . . ."

I fumbled for the mouse and clicked. A video popped up. A woman in a military helmet and a white, collared shirt smiled at me.

She took off the helmet and shook out a huge mass of stripy blonde hair. "Hi, I'm Janet March." Her teeth were so white they glowed. "If you're watching this, congratulations: you've avoided a major business catastrophe. But you're not out of the woods yet."

I'm not?

"Danger is everywhere."

It is?

"You *must* follow my patent-pending, four-point plan if you want to *crush* your competition. Are you ready?"

Yes.

"Good."

I looked to make sure Janet March wasn't standing behind me.

"Click the IDES buttons to learn more."

With a click, the screen turned into a map dotted with four points: I, D, E, and S. Each letter had its own icon: a lightbulb for the I, an equal sign with a line slashed through it for the D, a magnifying glass for the E, and a question mark for S. The S was marked "Your Final Destination."

A new video popped up.

"Welcome to the first day of the rest of your life," Janet March said. She now had bangs and was wearing a turtleneck. "I'll be blunt: I'm not here to sugarcoat anything for you. You're not a child, right?"

Well . . .

"Life's not some cozy playroom where everybody shares their toys," Janet said. "Have you ever been in a playroom? It's nonstop fighting."

She had a point.

"Competition happens when at least two parties strive for a goal that can't be shared," Janet continued. "In nature, competition occurs between organisms that live in the same environment."

"Or in the same cul-de-sac," I muttered.

"When we're young, we're taught to get along.

Especially you, ladies," Janet March said, pointing at the screen. I jumped. "That's called cooperation. But getting along doesn't get you anywhere. Competition is the *opposite* of cooperation. Competition is not evil, though. It's a good thing. It creates positive change, like better products and services. Monopolies, on the other hand, are *bad*."

What's so bad about a board game? I wondered.

"A monopoly occurs when there's no competition. One business holds all the power. In the long run, monopolists raise prices, reduce choice, and prevent innovation." She paused. "And they're *illegal*."

I gasped. Peter Presents was a monopoly. That made Peter Gronkowski a monopolist!

"Innovation is the *first* point in my four-point, patent-pending plan to crush the competition: The IDES of Janet March. Click 'I' to begin." She winked. "It's free!"

———·———

I printed every free guide on Janet March's website. With each word I read, I transformed into a more serious businesswoman. I pictured myself with bangs and a turtleneck.

The "I" in IDES stood for *Innovation*, I learned.

Janet March said Innovation meant creating something new and different.

The next step in IDES was *Differentiation*. How are you different from your competitor? "Being different is not enough," Janet wrote. "You have to be better."

That's where Janet March stopped. If you wanted to find out E and S, you had to pay $199.95 by check, money order, or credit card. Janet said this was a very reasonable price. Still, I didn't have close to that much money.

I spun Mom's ring around my thumb. If Peter sold rocks, what could I do to be innovative? Different? I had to sell something better than rocks.

That didn't seem too hard. Rocks were dirty, and you could find them anywhere.

Wooooh, Molly whimpered at my feet. She does that when she's bored.

I waved my hand around to entertain her. The ring made dancing lights on the wall like a kaleidoscope.

Molly ran in circles trying to chase them.

"Calm down, Molly," I said. "It's just pyrite."

Pyrite. I rolled the word around in my mouth.

"Pyrite," I said again. It sounded glamorous.

Dazzling. Much, much better than any rock Peter Gronkowski's intern could dig out of his backyard.

I held my ring up to the table lamp. It sparkled at me like it was winking.

Be resourceful, I reminded myself.

———————

Pyrite doesn't grow on trees or sprout in backyards, but I knew where to find it: the Super Stones corner of the Poplar Children's Museum gift shop. I'd hang out there on field trips while other kids raided the Dino-Mite action figures.

The next day after school, I stepped through the gleaming doors of the Poplar Children's Museum. I was turning toward the gift shop when something in the lobby caught my eye.

The Wily Wizard.

The Wily Wizard sat upon a throne in a glass box. He had been in the Poplar Children's Museum since before I was born. He wore a robe and a white turban wrapped around his head. When you put in a dollar, he'd spit out your fortune. His left eyebrow was arched.

Ugh. Is there anything Peter Gronkowski *doesn't* steal?

A bell rang when I stormed into the museum gift shop.

"Holler if you need anything," called the cashier.

I only needed one thing, and I found it quickly. Tucked away in an unassuming bin: a glistening, glittering pile of pyrite.

Each nugget was four dollars. I picked out the six chunkiest pieces and headed to the register.

"That'll be twenty-four bones," said the cashier. His name tag said Carlos.

I clutched my turtle change purse. Why was getting even so expensive? Oh well. It was worth it. I was making an investment in *me*.

For my entire life's savings, Carlos gave me a bag of pyrite, some change, and a receipt that said NO RETURNS OR EXCHANGES.

I shivered. It sounded so final.

CYRANO'S REVENGE

CHAPTER XLIX

Cyrano wept beside her parents' graves. Their modest shack had gone up in flames the very night Pouncey the nonpoet had betrayed her. A messenger had knocked on her pigpen stall, bearing the horrible news.

She raced home immediately, stricken with both grief and despair that she could not confront the cowardly criminal.

Sadly, Cyrano's sister Tulip could not be there to share in her sorrow. Tulip and Sir Michael the Strange were the proud new parents of quadruplets, and thus were unable to travel.

Cyrano laid her cheek upon the grass. Its dewy

coolness felt like ice against the fury coursing through her body. Deep inside, Cyrano wondered if her rage toward Pouncey had somehow ignited the fire that killed her parents.

"Pouncey, you worthless sub-pig!" she howled into the wind.

"Excuse me?" said a voice behind her.

Cyrano spun around. It was a knight.

"Please forgive me," Cyrano said, her face now burning from shame.

"Of course, m'lady," the knight said. "Are you Cyrano or Tulip, perchance?"

"I am Cyrano."

"Then I bring you news."

"Oh great. Now what?"

"You, m'lady, are of royal blood," the knight replied. "A member of the Introversia dynasty. Your parents did not want you to know until their death."

Cyrano gasped.

"My Queen," he said, kneeling. "How do you wish to rule your new kingdom?"

Peter Presents:
GRAND OPENING OF ROCKS ROCK!

THE WAIT IS OVER! From the creator of Star Maps of Poplar Lane and Fabulous Fortunes comes . . . ROCKS ROCK!

WHO: Peter Gronkowski, Rock Expert, CEO, CFO, COO, Entrepreneur, Emperor

WHAT: Rocks Rock!, a Stunning Display of Organic, Locally Sourced Rocks.

WHEN: Saturday, March 17 at 8:00 a.m.

WHERE: The Man Cave (aka the Curb Outside Peter Gronkowski's House)

WHY: Because You Rock.

P.S. This flier is good for ten cents off any rock with green in it (expires 11:59 p.m. on St. Patrick's Day).

13
PETER

Saturday, 7:47 a.m., Daniel wheeled the Peter Presents, Inc., Mobile Workplace onto the lawn. I hung back on the porch, surveying my empire.

The morning sun bounced off my black shades. I didn't even care that Dad got them at the Dollar Palace. Soon I'd have enough cash for bona fide Ray-Ban Wayfarers. The sidewalk glittered like it was paved with gold, or at least silicon carbide.

Daniel wasn't even getting on my nerves that much. Well, except he was wearing the leprechaun costume from his St. Patrick's Day preschool party. Ordinarily I request full wardrobe approval, but Mom flashed the Evil Eye when I complained.

I didn't sleep much last night. Standard preopening day jitters. Also, some amateur girls were having a sleepover next door. They talked and giggled all night. Then they woke up early to do it again.

I wouldn't let their unprofessional behavior stop me. Adrenaline and Happy Outlook cereal (generic) would keep me going. I even drank 2 percent milk out of my lucky Peter Presents, Inc., coffee cup.

 BUSINESS TIP: Use a coffee cup to look professional, even if you're not allowed to drink coffee yet.

"Stand on your tiptoes," I told Daniel. "Get that sign up high."

"I can't reach," Daniel whined.

Problem #1 with having a four-year-old intern: four-year-olds are short.

I gave Daniel a Corporate Boost. That means I held him up by the waist. Granddad gave me Corporate Boosts when I was too short to reach the filing cabinet in his office. My very first Peter Presents monogrammed loafers dangled off Daniel's toes. They were way too big for him, even though he'd worn three pairs of socks to make them fit.

After Daniel hung the sign, we stood back. PETER PRESENTS: ROCKS ROCK! sparkled above the Man Cave.

The Man Cave was a giant cardboard box. I'd cut jagged edges along the outside so it looked like a cave.

Problem #2 with having a four-year-old intern: your mom won't let him near scissors. My Featured Rocks sat at the front of the display, each with its own hand-written label. I wrote them myself, even though that was an amateur duty. Problems #3 and #4 with having a four-year-old intern: they can't read or write.

7:53 a.m. Dr. Spumoni pulled out of his garage in his new 6-series Midnight Metallic BMW. He gave me a thumbs-up like he always does on opening days. I nodded professionally. Daniel drew green suns on the sidewalk.

 BUSINESS TIP: Sidewalk chalk is professional as long as it's green.

8:30 a.m. Mel Chang was right on time.

"If it isn't my favorite Poplar Lane blogger," I greeted her like always.

"Oh . . . hi," she said.

I raised an eyebrow. Mel is supposed to say, "What's new?"

"I'm sure you're wondering what's new," I said. "All of it. You're the very first person to lay your eyes on my exclusive merchandise."

Mel nibbled a dark purple fingernail. Where was her phone?

"I'm ready for my interview," I said, getting us back on track. "My intern can set up the photo shoot." I wasn't sure he could. At that moment, my intern was worm hunting. I hoped Mel wouldn't mention his unprofessional behavior in her five-star review.

"Sorry," Mel said. "I'm going to see Gilda Stones."

"Who?" I asked. "I know everyone in this cul-de-sac. There's no Gilda Stones."

Mel rolled her eyes. "You know," she said. "The archaeologist." She nodded at the house next door.

This was not Mel's pattern. First, Mel was always my first customer. Second, she always took my picture. Third, in all our years of doing business, Mel Chang had never once mentioned archeologists.

And why was there an archeologist next door? Wait. Maybe that slumber party I heard wasn't a slumber party at all. Maybe it was an archeologist party. Mr. Chambers is a librarian. I bet he knows a lot of archeologists. They must have come into town for my Rocks Rock! opening.

It was all making sense.

"Oh, *that* Gilda Stones," I said. "The archeologist. Sure, sure. We have a meeting today. Tell her I said hi. I look forward to chatting later."

An endorsement from a real archeologist would go a long way toward cementing Rocks Rock! as the most successful Peter Presents, Inc., enterprise ever.

"Okay," said Mel.

"And take your time," I said in my most relaxed voice. "I'll set aside my highest quality quartz just for you."

"Perf," Mel said as she stomped past me.

My head was starting to sweat.

"Daniel," I said. "I need to know everything about Gilda Stones. What makes her tick? Write it all down. Wait. You can't write. Just remember it."

Daniel tapped his head. "Ticks."

Don't sell yourself short, I told myself. *You're a rock expert, too.*

I took a deep, cleansing breath to calm down. *One, two, three.* I smelled cut grass and lawn mower gas. Something was missing.

Lemonade.

The cul-de-sac was extra quiet. There weren't

even jackhammers going off at Ken's house. The only sound was Daniel singing a made-up song about worm pizza.

8:47 a.m. Mel Chang stomped out of the house next door.

"Intern," I said to Daniel, snapping my fingers. "My headset."

He was wearing my headset.

"Terrific," Daniel said. "I'll give you ten worms tomorrow, Tom."

I almost corrected him for playing with my expensive office equipment. But out of nowhere, I felt proud. Daniel was mirroring my behavior. A chip off the old block.

Stomp, stomp.

Mel was getting close.

I stepped in front of the booth, folded my hands into a Power Tent, and smiled at her.

She stomped right by me.

"Mel!" I said. "Don't forget your quartz."

"Sorry, Peter," she said. "I, uh, have to go to the mall."

The mall? First, the mall doesn't open till 10 a.m on Saturdays. Second, what about my opening day photo shoot? My interview?

Before I could say anything, she was halfway down the street, tapping on her phone.

Calling after customers is not professional, so I didn't do it.

Instead, I peeled the "On Hold for Mel C" sticker off the quartz.

"Rocks for sale!" Daniel shouted, shimmying in front of the booth. His cries bounced all over the nearly empty cul-de-sac.

I did ten Juiced-Up Jumping Jacks and five Deep Dive Lunges.

I took an urgent sales call on my headset.

I settled into my Executive Lawn Chair and caught up on the latest *Mind Your Business*.

 BUSINESS TIP: Panic is not productive.

9:26 a.m. Mike the Unusual crossed the street. I stood up and waved. He saluted me.

Finally. My first customer.

He turned up the sidewalk to the house next door.

Why was Mike the Unusual meeting with Gilda Stones?

The sun beat down on my neck. I peeled off my sweaty leather jacket. Daniel put it on.

"Peter, I'm thirsty," he said. "I want lemon—"

"Don't say it," I warned him. "Water only."

"Water is boring," Daniel announced. "I'm hungry!"

To tell you the truth, my stomach was growling like Count App E. Tite's in the movie *Predator Intestines*. But I hadn't earned a Success Snack. It's my incentive, and it's not for small-timers who can't move product on a Saturday morning. If I didn't get one, neither did Daniel.

I crossed my arms. When Daniel saw that I wouldn't budge, he pouted and sat on the curb. He put his head down on his knees. His curls bounced as he tapped his feet to an imaginary beat.

Hunger was already making Daniel lose his mind. He shouldn't have to starve just because I was failing as a professional.

"Fine," I said. Maybe watching him eat would motivate me to do better.

Daniel ran into the house. He came back carrying a Little Buster's brownie and a glass of 2 percent milk. Mmmmm. I could almost taste that perfect, successful combination of flavors on my tongue.

My stomach growled even louder. Tom Reddi says you should always be hungry. If you're not hungry, you should be worried.

I was hungry, but I was still worried. Something was wrong. And it wasn't just my empty stomach.

I should have been on top of the world. I was outside, in my Executive Lawn Chair, and in my element: selling. But in all my days as a business professional, I had never gone a whole morning without making a sale.

9:40 a.m. Mike the Unusual came out of the house next door.

I slipped on my headset. "Thank you for the kind words about my business, Mr. Reddi," I said, loud enough for Mike to hear.

Mike put big blue headphones over his curly hair and walked by me just like Mel.

"Wait!" I yelled. I started to run after him.

I screeched to a halt. Did I yell? Was I *running*?

Mike pushed one of his earpieces to the side. "Yeah?"

"Uh . . . what are you listening to?" I asked.

"Amusing Illusions. It's the number one comedy-slash-magic podcast. I've got a gig coming up."

"Rock on," I said. *Nice rebound*, I thought. *And nice job working the brand right into the conversation.* "So, what kind of rock are you in the market for today?"

"Sorry, man. I already bought a rock today."

I laughed. "Good one. I've been out here all morning. You didn't buy a rock today."

Mike blinked. Even though Mike was a comedian/magician-in-training, he didn't really kid around.

"I didn't buy it from you," he said. He readjusted his headphones and started off again.

"*Wait!*" I grabbed his arm. "Can I see the rock?"

Mike reached into his pocket and pulled out something chunky and gold.

"What is it?" I asked. It looked expensive.

"Pyrite, dude," he said.

My heart beat in my throat like it was trying to choke me. "Who sold it to you?" I asked.

Mike blinked again. "Gilda Stones," he said. "You know. Rachel Chambers."

EL DORADO, the Lost City of Gold
(A 4-D Interactive Adventure)
EXCLUSIVE *CLASSY*

Dear Exclusive Customer,

Do you think standing around a booth is boring? Are you unimpressed by dirty rocks? Offended by the term "Man Cave"? Pan for pyrite at El Dorado, the Lost City of Gold (A 4-D Interactive Adventure).*

Need a high-quality, eye-catching gift for that special someone? When ordinary won't do, visit El Dorado, the Lost City of Gold (A 4-D Interactive Adventure).

EL DORADO, the Lost City of Gold
(a 4-D Interactive Adventure):
Saturday, March 17 ✽ 8:30 a.m.
Backyard of 9045 Poplar Lane ✽ 555-672-4762

Best Wishes and Golden Dreams,
Dr. Gilda Stones **

* Pyrite is not real gold. I would never lie to customers. Not like some people in this cul-de-sac.

** Dr. Gilda Stones is also known as Rachel Chambers, CEO of Rachel Rules Enterprises. She is not known as Puppet.

14

Rachel

My alarm blared into the darkness.

Opening day!

I tapped the snoring sleeping bag by my bed. "Clover!" I whispered.

"*Garrpppphhhh . . . splurgggg,*" Clover moaned. We'd been up almost all night.

"We have thirty-seven minutes." I checked the clock again. "Thirty-six." Being a business professional meant I'd have to start getting more serious about time. And I didn't even have an official timepiece like Peter's.

I grabbed the alarm clock. I'd just have to carry it with me all day. Lucky for me it ran on batteries. *Now that's being resourceful,* I thought.

While Clover buried her face in a pillow, I changed into my costume.

I buttoned up a purple blouse from Mom's trunk and tucked my jeans into tall black rain boots. Then I put on Mom's pyrite ring.

I stood in front of the mirror. Rachel, unpaid intern, was no more. I was Dr. Gilda Stones, lead El Dorado archaeologist. Like Indiana Jones, but not afraid of snakes. Especially not snakes named Peter Gronkowski.

"Okay, stay in bed," I told Clover. "I'll put the glitter on the sidewalk without you."

She shot up like a rocket. "Glitter!"

"Then come on!" I said.

Clover threw on the top half of her mom's gold silky pajamas, so long on her it was like a dress. She added a gold sparkly belt and gold clip-on earrings.

"Anastasia Emerald, Archeologist Support Professional, at your service," Clover said, twirling around. "Isn't this something?"

"Uh . . . yeah," I said

Anastasia Emerald is Clover's favorite name. When we play detective agency, she's Anastasia Emerald, P.I. Teenage battle mermaids? Anastasia Emerald, Sergeant-at-Fins. She even convinced the Poplar Middle School crossing guard that it was her real name.

Clover finished applying her third coat of gold lip gloss and smacked her lips together. "Ready, boss!" she said, saluting me.

Boss. My skin tingled. It felt good and scary at the same time.

We raced downstairs. Before we tiptoed outside, I poked my head out the front door to check for any sign of Peter. Nothing.

Clover sprinkled a glitter arrow on the driveway pointing to my front door.

When we went back inside, I found a note on the kitchen island:

Dear Scoots,

Sorry I won't be around today. I'll be thinking of you. The poet Robert Frost once said, "Nothing gold can stay." But the poet Dad says, "Pyrite is forever."

Love, Dad.

I tucked his note into my belt.

"Oh!" Clover said. She flew up the stairs then came back down. "I got you a present." She handed me a can of Midas All-Weather Spray Paint in Solid Gold. "It's from my collection!"

Clover is an artist, so art supplies are a big deal to her. I gave her a huge hug.

We walked to the back door.

"Ready?" Clover asked.

I took a deep breath. "Ready," I said.

The door creaked as I pushed it open. There it was: El Dorado, the Lost City of Gold. Gold glitter sparkled on top of Lake Guatavita (a baby pool, courtesy of Clover). Pans were piled high in stacks around the water.

"Your business is sooooo cool!" Clover said.

"Interactive experience," I reminded her. I imagined Janet March resting a proud hand on my shoulder.

I scattered a handful of plain rocks in the water. Then I dropped in the pyrite. As a final touch, I sprinkled grass all over the top of the water to make it look more mysterious.

"Where's the real El Dorado?" Clover asked as she arranged palm leaves around the pool.

"Colombia," I said. "Well, kind of. The real El Dorado was a native Muisca chief. He covered his body in gold dust and jumped into Lake Guatavita to offer gold to the gods."

"Ooooh," she said. I could tell she was imagining herself covered in gold dust.

"Then the conquistadores came," I said. "They heard stories about gold and thought El Dorado was a place. They drained Lake Guatavita and stole a lot of the Muisca's treasures. They also killed people. All of that to find a city that wasn't even real."

Clover stopped arranging the leaves. "That's awful," she said. "How do you know so much about it?"

"It's my ancient myth project for school," I said.

"Gosh," Clover said. It takes a lot to make her quiet. "The conquistadores sound even worse than Peter."

"Yeah," I said.

I stood back. Peter's house seemed extra dark beside all the shimmer in my backyard.

"There's no room for guilt in competition," Janet March would tell me. My secret business gave me a competitive advantage. Still, I felt . . . sneaky.

"So if we're archaeologists," Clover said, "but the El Dorado place isn't real . . . what are customers trying to find?"

"Pyrite," I said. "We're just imagining it's real. It's part of the interactive experience."

"Okay," Clover said. "As long as we're not conquistadores."

We went inside to eat. Clover and I toasted waffles and watched my alarm clock. 8:26. 8:27.

"You don't want to carry that clock around all day," Clover said. "I have an idea!"

She ran into my garage and came back with a jump rope. She looped the rope around the clock a few times and put it on her shoulder.

"See? It's an alarm-clock purse! Or whatever archaeologists use," she said.

"It can be my satchel."

8:29. 8:30.

Ding-dong! I've been workin' on the railroad! Ding-dong!

"The door!" Clover yelled. She sprinted down the hall and checked the peephole. "It's Mel Chang!" She opened the door.

"Am I first?" Mel asked.

"Yes," I said, running up behind Clover.

"Perf," she said. She narrowed her eyes and scanned me top to bottom. "Sick belt, Gilda. What's new?"

A compliment from Mel Chang? I almost passed out from shock.

"That's *Dr.* Gilda," Clover said. She winked at me.

I led Mel through the house to the backyard. "Behold . . . El Dorado!" I told her.

It takes a lot to impress Mel Chang, but I swear, for a half second, she smiled. Then her face snapped back, and she was all business. "I'll need a few pics," she said. "With you in them."

Some people have nightmares about going to school naked. I have nightmares about picture day. In every yearbook photo, my face looks like I'm sitting on burning coals.

"You can do it, Dr. Stones!" Clover whispered.

I breathed in my name. I wasn't Rachel Chambers, picture-phobic nobody. I was Dr. Gilda Stones, archaeologist. *Lead* archaeologist. Gilda Stones definitely loved the spotlight.

I opened my eyes, tilted my chin up, and smiled as Mel clicked away.

"Okay, let's pan," Mel said.

"Uh . . . sure!" I said. "My assistant will get you started."

"Your assistant?" Clover asked. "Oh, right! That's me!" She picked up a clipboard and put a pen behind her ear.

"One turn is five dollars," Clover said in her I'm-in-charge voice, the one she uses to make her sister change the baby's diaper. "You get three chances per turn to find pyrite. But you only get to keep one piece of pyrite, even if you find more. If you don't find pyrite by your third turn, that's it."

"Five dollars?" Mel asked, raising an eyebrow. Could everyone in the world raise an eyebrow but me? I needed to up my training. "I get the fifty percent media discount, right, Gilda?" She paused. "That's what Peter does."

"Uh, sure," I said. "I guess."

Mel kneeled and skimmed her pan along the top of the water. "It's just grass," she said, squinting. "And glitter."

"That counts as your first turn!" Clover announced.

"Try scooping," I said, forcing a smile.

Mel scooped, this time going deeper. "It's a rock," she announced. Then she yawned.

"Last chance!" Clover said.

My blouse stuck to my skin. Was my first Mel Chang review going to end in one star?

Mel scooped with all her might. She pulled up a sparkling chunk of pyrite.

"Yes," I whispered.

"Score!" yelled Clover.

Mel grinned. This time it was a real, actual smile. "It's totes gorg," she said. That seemed like a good thing.

Mel started to leave, then turned to me on her way out. "Expect my review this afternoon. Oh yeah. And Peter says hi."

My stomach balled up into a knot. "What?" I said. How did he know about El Dorado already? Was he angry?

"Squeeeee!" Clover said after Mel left. "She's totally giving you five stars! Are you psyched?" When Clover gets excited, she turns into a wind-up toy. "What should we do with the $2.50? I have soooo many ideas!"

"Oh," I said. I hadn't really thought about money. I mean, it was technically mine. But Clover was my assistant. She had helped, too. And I wasn't Peter. I was a good boss. I took care of my employees.

"We can split it," I said.

"Awesome!" said Clover. "You're the best boss ever."

We toasted more waffles and talked about Peter's message.

"If he comes here, I'll be your security," Clover said. "He's *not* getting past Anastasia Emerald."

Just as I squeezed the syrup bottle, the doorbell rang again. I held my breath as Clover got up and ran down the hall. When she came back to the kitchen, her eyes were as big as beach balls.

"Mike the Unusual," she whispered, even though her whisper is a normal person's regular voice.

I exhaled.

"How's my hair?" Clover asked as we raced to meet Mike.

"Be professional," I said. Clover opened the door slowly and dramatically, like she was revealing a secret passage to Mars.

"Hellooooo." She batted her eyelashes at Mike so hard when she greeted him that I felt a breeze.

"Is there a bug in your eye?" Mike asked.

"She's fine," I said. "Come in."

"Here, I'll show you where to go," said Clover, grabbing his hand. I rolled my eyes.

In the backyard, Clover went over the panning rules. This time she sounded like she was reciting a love poem.

Mike scored a piece of pyrite on the first try.

"You're a natural!" squealed Clover.

"Nice," Mike said. He dried the pyrite on his shirt and put it in his pocket. "Oh, I almost forgot." He reached into his other pocket. His hand came out empty.

"My invisible business card," he said. "From one business owner to another."

I reached out, pretending to take it. He doesn't call himself Mike the Unusual for nothing.

"It's invisible because I'm a magician," he explained. "It says I'm available for birthday parties, weddings, special events, and bar and bat mitzvahs. It was hard to fit all of that on one card."

"Birthday parties?" Clover said. "*My* birthday party is April 1."

"Uh, Clover," I said. "I'm sure Mike is busy—"

"I would be honored," Mike said.

Clover turned redder than her hair.

After Mike left, Clover grabbed my arm.

"You are so lucky he gave you an invisible business card," she said. "Treasure it. I would kiss it every night."

"How do you kiss—"

"*Wait!*" someone yelled outside.

"What was that?" I asked. We ran to the living room to look out the window.

Outside Peter was grabbing Mike the Unusual's arm. Mike pulled something out of his pocket and gave it to Peter.

I dug my fingernails into my palms. It wasn't an invisible business card. It was pyrite. *My* pyrite.

15
PETER

I squeezed the pyrite in my fist.

There was no Dr. Gilda Stones.

"You bought *this* pyrite," I said to Mike, "from *that* Rachel Chambers?" I pointed to her house.

"Indeed," Mike said. "At El Dorado, the 4-D Interactive Experience. Didn't you get the invite?"

What invite?

 BUSINESS TIP: Pretend to know what's going on at all times, even when you don't.

I nodded. "Right, the invite." I gave the pyrite back to Mike.

"So I'm broke now," Mike said. "No more rocks for me."

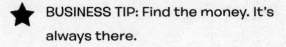

BUSINESS TIP: Find the money. It's always there.

When someone says they don't have money, you're supposed to answer their objections. It's Business 101.

"Hoo-hoo-ha. I think there's been a misunderstanding," I said. "These aren't ordinary rocks."

Mike raised his eyebrows. Not everyone can raise just one. It's a special skill.

"Are they magic?" he asked.

"No," I said. "They're investment pieces."

"Nice," he said. "So they get more valuable over time?"

"Sure, maybe," I said. "Are you familiar with our Peter Presents Payment Plan?"

Mike shrugged. "Nah," he said. "I'm good."

I should have asked him to share his concerns about the price. I wish I'd said, "I'm sorry you're having money troubles." That works because the person will say, "I'm not having money troubles!" and get money to prove they're not poor.

But what did I do?

I shook his hand.

I let him go.

Snap out of it, Peter. I slapped myself on the cheek as Mike walked away.

My skin felt hot and uncomfortable, like it didn't belong to me. It belonged to an amateur.

I scratched my wrist under my watch. My right hand, the one I'd used to shake Mike's, was covered in gold glitter.

"Peter, don't hit your face," Daniel said. "That's not nice. I'm telling. And what's pyrite?"

"Trash," I said, marching up to the front door. "I'm washing this glitter off. Just hold down the fort."

"I'm not supposed to be alone!" Daniel yelled after me.

Mom met me in the hallway.

"Peter, where's Daniel? He's not supposed to be—" Her face turned super white, like the most deluxe printer paper at Office Depot. "Honey, what's wrong?"

"Nothing," I said. "Business is terrific! Everything is terrific!"

She grabbed both my hands. "You're breaking out in hives. Looks like an allergic reaction. It's on your cheek, too." She chewed her bottom lip. "Hm. Dr. Spumoni has Saturday hours."

"It's opening day," I said slowly. "I'm not leaving

my business. On opening day. For a doctor."

"This is your health, Peter."

"But—"

"No buts."

"But my business!"

"I'm your mother," she said. "Your health is my business."

"That doesn't make sense!" I said. "You're a lawyer! Your business is law!"

"Rick!" Mom yelled over her shoulder.

"You rang?" Dad called from upstairs.

"Will you sit outside with Daniel and watch Peter's booth? I need to run Peter over to Dr. Spumoni."

Dad plodded downstairs like a giant demon boulder from an old Scare TV movie called *The Giant Demon Boulder*. It was slow, but it destroyed everything in its path.

To run a business, you need drive, ambition, and killer instinct. Dad has a killer instinct for Japanese beetles in the tomato patch.

He saw my face and cringed. "Oooh. Feel better, bud. Daniel and I, we've got this."

Dad and Daniel. Running my business. *This* was the horror movie. I wished someone would cover my eyes. They were swelling shut, anyway.

Mom shuffled me into her 1998 pre-certified Honda Civic.

"Why is there glitter everywhere?" she muttered, turning the key in the ignition.

Daniel waved at us as Mom shifted into reverse. He was saying something. I rolled down the window.

"Don't get shot in the butt!" he yelled.

I shrunk down in my seat. Last year I got sick on vacation. I had to go to an emergency clinic. The doctor gave me an antibiotic shot in the rear end. Now Daniel thinks that happens every time I go to the doctor.

If anyone in the cul-de-sac knew that, my reputation would be ruined.

As we pulled away, I saw Daniel and Dad in the rearview mirror. They were playing catch. With my merchandise. Catch.

———•———

Diagnosis: I, Peter Gronkowski, was allergic to glitter.

"Not glitter exactly," Dr. Spumoni explained to Mom. "Allergies can be tough to pin down. Could be the mica in the glitter." He turned to me. "*Mica* is the mineral in glitter that makes it *sparkle*."

Dr. Spumoni is normal at his house and in the cul-de-sac, but he uses an annoying baby voice at work. Didn't medical school teach doctors to treat patients professionally? Patients are their customers. "A *mineral* is—"

"I know what a mineral is," I replied. "I'm a rock professional." I maintained eye contact until he checked his chart.

"So, Peter, are you part of this *chess club* craze?" Dr. Spumoni asked me.

"Huh?"

He looked up from his chart. "Maybe it's a Poplar Prep thing. Ken and his buddies are really into it."

My face got hot. It wasn't the allergic reaction. Hearing about Poplar Prep reminded me how low my PP fund was, and how far away I was from Ken and his "buddies." Not that I cared about chess. Tom Reddi never once mentioned it in the Power Pastimes section of *Mind Your Business*.

Mom tapped her phone. "You know," she said, "I'm allergic to mica in makeup. Maybe it runs in the family."

Dr. Spumoni waved his finger at the tip of my nose. "No more playing with glitter, Peter. And absolutely no makeup!" He threw his head back and howled.

I didn't laugh to mirror his behavior. I didn't even smile.

Dr. Spumoni tore a sheet off his notepad. "This cream will help the itching," he told Mom. "You can also give him some Benadryl." He turned to me. "*Benadryl* will make you *very* sleepy. No operating large machinery, young man!"

Mom and I left the doctor's office.

"I'm not taking Benadryl," I told Mom in the car. "I can't afford to sleep." She raised an eyebrow.

At the pharmacy, I calculated my profit and loss for the day. The time I lost at the doctor was going to hurt. Mom argued with the pharmacist about something called a copay.

As we pulled up to the house, I followed the thickest glitter path with my eyes. It led to Rachel Chambers's front door.

Dad was leaning all the way back in my Executive Lawn Chair. One good thing: the booth hadn't burned down.

"Hey!" he called. "Danny Boy's down for the count." He pointed to Daniel, who was snoring on a giant pile of pillows. "How're you feeling, Peter?"

"He's allergic to glitter," Mom answered for me.

"Mom," I said. "Please keep it down. What's with the pillows?"

"Daniel said you wanted him to build a fort," Dad said.

"What? No," I said. "I told him to hold down the . . . never mind. I need numbers. How many customers?"

He shrugged. "Hard to say. A few stopped by to browse, though."

 BUSINESS TIP: Browsing is the enemy.

Dad had zero training in how to close a sale. I pictured dollar signs walking by the booth and Dad waving as they walked away.

"A lot of kids went next door," Dad said. Just then, Scott MacGregor walked out of Rachel Chambers's house. He had a giant grin on his glittery face.

I scanned my merchandise. The Quality Quartz was missing.

"Did Mel Chang come back?" I asked.

"Hm, not sure. I don't think so. Maybe?"

"That's not helpful," I said. "My star item is gone."

"Oh, right," Dad said. He snapped his fingers. "Danny Boy sold it!"

Huh. I knew some day the kid would come through. All he needed was strong leadership and a positive, employed role model.

"How much?" I asked. "Was there a bidding war?"

"Not exactly," Dad said. He winked. "He gave it to Daisy O'Reilly."

"Gave," I repeated. The word tasted like poison. "Gave. As in, no money exchanged for goods and services."

"Right," Dad said, standing up to stretch. "It was a wedding present. He said they got married under the big slides last week. Remember to tell him he did a good job, okay?"

A good job. Unbelievable.

I sat down in the Executive Lawn Chair. "Thanks for your help," I said. "I'll take it from here."

"No, sir," Mom said. "You need to be inside taking it easy."

I gripped the armrests tight.

"Relax, Peter," Dad said, squeezing my shoulder. "I'll keep an eye on things."

Relax. That was easy for him to say. He didn't

have almost-empty investment jars stashed under his desk. He didn't even have a desk anymore.

Selling isn't relaxing. It's not keeping an eye on things. It's an art. It's survival.

Mom waited by the front door. Her Evil Eye told me I had no choice. I had to go inside.

Dad saluted me as I walked up to the house.

I went right into Mom's office and pulled up Mel Chang's blog on her computer.

The front page showed a photo of someone wearing purple. "El Dorado," the caption said. "A FIVE STAR 4-D Interactive Experience NOT to be missed."

Five. Stars.

I squinted. The purple person was my former intern.

"Today is a sick joke," I said out loud to no one.

 BUSINESS TIP: Amateurs can be intimidated. Professionals cannot.

I walked calmly and professionally into the kitchen. "Mom?" I asked. "What's that thing when you send a letter to make someone stop doing something?"

She peeked out from behind a mountain of papers. "Oh," she said. "A cease-and-desist letter?"

"Yes!" I said. *Mind Your Business* ran a fascinating story on crafting the perfect cease-and-desist letter. Tom Reddi sent them to all the nearby ice cream stores before he opened the Cone Zone. It must have worked. Now he's the only one in Poplar. He made everyone disappear.

I went back to Mom's computer.

Later, Mom came in with a tray. "Famous Chicken Soup, 2 percent milk, and one Benadryl coming up!" Mom doesn't cook much. Her Famous Chicken Soup comes out of a can. It's "famous" because she puts sour cream on top.

She set the tray on the desk and kissed the top of my head. Good thing no customers were around to see that.

As she closed the office door behind her, my stomach growled. I'd missed both my Success Snack and my working lunch.

I tested a spoonful of soup. Not bad. I slurped a little more, then a lot. With every sip, my mind and body started to relax. But not the way Dad relaxes. My relaxation told me, "Peter, you're in control."

Rachel Chambers was an amateur. What was I worried about? This was one day in my entire lifetime of success.

"Don't forget your itch cream!" Mom yelled from the kitchen.

I groaned. I wasn't allergic to mica or glitter. I was allergic to being a loser. There was no cream for that.

I saved the file I was working on and hit Print. Soon everything would be normal again, the way it was supposed to be. No competition.

I eyed the tiny pink Benadryl on the tray. I'd earned it. I gulped it down with my 2 percent milk.

Daniel barged in a while later. I was so relaxed I didn't even tell him to knock first.

"Peter! I made you a card," Daniel said. He gave me a piece of folded paper with a smiling sun saying, "Get Well Soon!" That part was obviously written by Dad. But Daniel signed his name. He also signed for Mo, his stuffed monkey. "And I sold a rock!"

"It's beautiful," I said, hugging the card to my chest. My head felt fuzzy and my eyelids were droopy. The Benadryl was kicking in. "You're a great intern. The best. I have another job for you." I handed him the cease-and-desist letter. "Take this to Rachel Chambers. It's a very special secret mission. That means don't tell Mom and Dad."

Daniel nodded.

"Dannn-iel." The words felt slippery coming out of my mouth. I squeezed his hand. "Watching you grow. It's like . . . seeing myself . . . hatch . . . from a golden egg."

"You came from a golden egg?" Daniel asked.

"Go forth, my brother," I said with a yawn.

"Okay, boss!" He ran out of the office.

Boss. Hearing that word made my amateur itching melt away.

Every great general needs a team, I thought as I wandered upstairs to my room. *Maybe I should lie down. Or maybe I'll take a bath. With oatmeal. Mom says it's good for rashes.*

"Ha," I snorted, picturing myself eating oatmeal in the bathtub. "Ha."

I sank into my bed. The sheets smelled clean. The pillows felt soft. I just needed a . . . Power . . . Nap . . .

16

Rachel

I emptied my turtle change purse onto the kitchen table.

Thirty-two dollars and fifty cents. An eight dollar and fifty cent profit on my very first day as a professional businesswoman!

There was just one problem. All my pyrite was gone.

I checked my satchel clock. 4:01 p.m. The Children's Museum closed in fifty-nine minutes.

I grabbed my money and sprinted faster than I ever did in gym class. While I ran, I did some math in my head (Janet March called that "multitasking"). I could still afford only eight pieces of pyrite, but it was better than nothing.

On the way back home, I remembered my promise to Clover to split the profits. But you have to spend money to make money. From what I've read, that's how business works. She would understand.

———•———

"Join the track team, Scoots?" Dad asked as I came into the kitchen, huffing and puffing. "That's great! Experts recommend team sports for socialization."

"Nope," I said. "Business is hard work. And good exercise."

After Dad and I ate chicken Parmesan penne and cleaned up the kitchen, the doorbell rang. I opened the door to find a leprechaun on my front porch.

"Hi, Puppet!" Daniel Gronkowski said. "Special delivery from Peter!" He handed me a folded piece of paper. The words CEASE AND DESIST glared at me, in red marker.

"What's this?" I asked.

Daniel shrugged. "I can't read."

"Where's Peter?" I asked.

"Asleep."

It wasn't even dark yet. If I could raise an eyebrow, I would have.

I opened the letter: "Notice of violation. You are violating a neighborhood code by pouring glitter on sidewalks."

Neighborhood code?

"Real doctors have shown that glitter causes allergies. Therefore, you're a threat to public health. We strongly urge you to cease and desist El Dorado (A 4-D Interactive Experience), effective today."

"Cease" means stop. On the second day of fourth grade, Ms. Ryan put a CEASE THE CHATTER sign up in our classroom. She pointed to it when she wanted kids to stop talking (usually Clover). I wasn't sure about desist, but I could put it together well enough. Peter wanted me to shut down El Dorado.

There was more: "By sending this friendly notice, my client, Peter Gronkowski (Founder, CEO, CFO, COO, Entrepreneur, Innovator, Emperor) hopes he won't have to sue you. Best, Diana Sharpe-Gronkowski, JD." A 10 percent off coupon for any Peter Presents, Inc., Rocks Rock! purchase was stapled to the bottom of the page. It was expired.

This was no "friendly notice." This was a threat.

I felt leprechaun eyes watching me closely.

"Thanks," I told Daniel. Dad says you shouldn't shoot the messenger because it's not their fault.

"Okay," Daniel said. "Bye, Puppet!"

I shut the door, searching the letter for clues. Would Peter's mom actually sue me if I kept El Dorado open? I pictured myself in handcuffs, and Mrs. Gronkowski standing before a judge, screaming, "She poured glitter, your honor!"

No, I decided as I marched into the kitchen. Did Peter think I was that big of an idiot? Didn't Mrs. Gronkowski have better things to do, like put murderers in prison?

Peter sent a four-year-old to do his dirty work. He couldn't even do it to my face.

I paced around the kitchen table, hoping it would make my brain slow down. It didn't work.

I sat down and ran my finger along the smooth, raised shell of my turtle change purse. Turtles. They don't get any respect. I would know. They're nice and quiet, but all anyone ever says is that they're slow.

Like the tortoise in "The Tortoise and the Hare." The tortoise was a nice guy who just wanted to run a race. The mean hare laughed at him. The hare thought he was better than everyone else, just like Peter. He was so sure he would win that he fell asleep in the middle of the race. The tortoise kept going and won.

He won.

I stood up.

This isn't the end, Peter Gronkowski. You think

you can threaten me and make me go away? You stirred the tortoise in her shell. Slow and steady wins the race. I will beat you. I will win.

Dad's office was empty, so I had the computer all to myself. I quickly typed my own letter for Peter and went to the kitchen to make him a very special gift.

Daniel was still outside when I stepped out into the blazing red sunset. He was dangling a worm over his mouth.

"Daniel!" I called. "Special delivery for Peter!"

CYRANO'S REVENGE

CHAPTER LVII

"My first act as Queen shall be to feed the poor!" said Queen Cyrano.

The crowd cheered.

"And every apprentice shall be paid and given proper credit for their work!" said Queen Cyrano.

The crowd cheered louder.

"And I demand more humane treatment of animals . . . especially cows! And pigs!"

A chorus of moos and oinks could be heard amid the joyous shouts.

"O, gracious one!" cried an old woman in rags. "How long we've waited for a fair, just, and female leader like your majesty."

"To be fair and just, I must punish those who betray me," Queen Cyrano continued. "It is the natural order of things." She paused. "Guards, bring forth Pouncey the phony poet."

The disgraced crook Pouncey knelt before Queen Cyrano. His once clean, freckle-free face was soiled with disgusting sweat.

"Pouncey, you are charged with committing Grand Word Theft," said Queen Cyrano. She turned to the jury of pigs beside her. "Pigs, is this the man, nay, the creature, who crept into our pigpen to steal my poetry?"

Cyrano's loyal pig witnesses oinked with all their might.

"Then it is so," Cyrano said. "I sentence you, Pouncey the Subpig, to Death's Door Prison!"

17
PETER

I opened my eyes. The sun hit my face.

Sun?

6:48 a.m.

I sat up in bed, feeling weird. Foggy. I remembered eating my mom's soup and taking Benadryl. Benadryl. It must have worked. I'd never fallen asleep without counting dollar signs before.

Then I remembered something about eggs. Oatmeal. I must be having breakfast dreams again.

My stomach rumbled. Thinking about money and breakfast always makes me hungry. I'd need a giant Success Breakfast this morning. Today was a brand-new day.

 BUSINESS TIP: Every professional has setbacks. It's not how many times

you get knocked down. It's how many
times you get back up.

I walked downstairs, taking extra-large steps.

"Peter, my man!" Dad said as I came into the kitchen. "Your face looks better. Less puffy. How are you feeling, bud?"

I pulled my green Peter Presents bowl down from its hiding place, behind the other bowls where Daniel can't reach it.

"On top of the world," I said, dumping out heaps of Happy Outlook cereal.

"Excellent," Dad said. He pointed at the calendar on the wall. "So, eight more days of spring break. I'm trying out some new cookie recipes for book club. You can be my official taste-tester. What else? Want to do anything fun?"

"Fun?" I almost choked on a shamrock marshmallow. "I'm working, Dad. Remember?"

"Right." Dad smiled as he stood up. "Let me know if you get a break. We could go to the park . . . collect rocks or something."

He was trying. But "collecting rocks" was a hobby. A business is not a hobby. And breaks are earned. They're not guaranteed.

I was getting more and more concerned about Dad's lack of motivation. First, you can't put "made book club cookies" on a résumé. Hiring managers would not be impressed. Second, it meant I had to pick up his slack even more than I already was.

"Daniel," I said. "Did you deliver my very important message?"

Daniel nodded, bits of Choco Crispy Sensations stuck to his face. I patted him on the shoulder. "Uh-huh!" he said. "She has a present for you, too." He zipped out of the room.

Odd, I thought. Tom Reddi says you're never supposed to gift up. That means don't give presents to your boss. It was probably just an apology for her unprofessional behavior.

Daniel came back with a shiny purple bag.

 BUSINESS TIP: Executives don't accept, sign for, or open deliveries. Those are low-level assistant duties.

"Go ahead," I told him.

Daniel reached into the bag. He pulled out a bottle of lemonade.

My stomach lurched.

"Yummy!" Daniel said.

Lemonade. The drink of *amateurs*.

"Get that out of my sight," I said. "Dump it down the drain."

"I can't," he said. "Twisty caps hurt my hand."

I put on Dad's rubber dish gloves and gave the cap a hard turn. Little yellow drops scattered all over the floor.

"Now dump it." I tiptoed around the disgusting puddles.

Daniel climbed the kitchen stool and poured the poison down the drain. I held my breath so I wouldn't inhale its nasty odor.

"Throw away the bottle," I said. "And the bag."

Daniel shook the bag and looked inside. "There's a note in there!" he said.

Still wearing rubber gloves, I pulled out the note. A baby carrot was taped to the bottom. The note said:

Enjoy your snack! Sincerely, The Tortoise.

The Tortoise? Lemonade? A baby carrot?

Rachel Chambers was messing with my head. This wasn't business. It was personal.

7:03 a.m. I went upstairs in search of my latest issue of *Mind Your Business*. I had fifty-seven minutes to get back into Professional Mode and zero time for amateur mind games.

"Business Is War" stretched across the cover in big red letters. As always, Tom Reddi had perfect timing.

I went right to the first article: "Know Your Competition." It was guest-written by Tom's friend Buster Landry, owner of Buster's Coffee.

"Competition is a natural part of business," Buster began.

I almost spit out my 2 percent milk. First, I don't have any competition. That word is not in my vocabulary. Second, competition isn't "natural." There are natural professionals, and there are amateurs.

Out of respect for Tom's friendship with Buster, I skimmed to the end.

"Listen to Sun Tzu, a Chinese general from 500 BC: 'Keep your friends close and your enemies closer.' Don't let obsession stop you from moving forward."

Terrible advice. What did some guy from 500 BC know, anyway? I wasn't keeping my enemy any closer than she already was. She was my neighbor. That was close enough.

I flipped to Tom's Redditorial, the opinion piece on the last page of every issue. I knew it would be good from the first line:

"If you ask me, monopolies get a bad rap."

Finally, some real wisdom. Why is a monopoly so bad? If someone is a better businessperson, why shouldn't they be on top? Why do people hate when other people are powerful? A monopoly means you're the best. Why should someone be punished for being the best?

"It all starts in B school," Tom wrote. "They teach you that competition is about price, quality, and service. It's all holding hands and kumbaya and fair play.

"But what's fair about business?" Tom continued. "Business is war. You're competing for limited resources: Other People's Money. Those are the spoils. Don't just get your hands dirty. Dig in. Get your fingernails dirty, too."

Tom Reddi was the smartest man alive.

"Don't give your competitors a choice," Tom wrote. "Just win. Worse comes to worse, you buy them out. What's their price? Everyone has one. Launch a hostile takeover. Take it. It's yours."

"It's mine," I said out loud.

18

Rachel

6:42 a.m. Sunday. My satchel alarm clock beeped on my tummy.

I hopped out of bed and ran to the window.

El Dorado was still there. My panning stream still glittered.

I sat down, feeling dizzy. What did I expect? Graffiti? Grand theft? All I knew was that I sent Peter Gronkowski lemonade, and actions have consequences.

That's the problem with revenge: You're always watching your back. You never know when the other person might make the next move.

I went downstairs and refreshed Mel Chang's blog for the forty-fifth time since yesterday. My five-star review was still there, too. So was my name, and my picture (even though Clover photobombed it with peace signs in the background).

7:12 a.m. I was picking berries out of my fruit salad when Clover called.

"Whoa," I said. "You're awake?"

"I couldn't sleep last night," Clover replied. Her voice sounded like gravel. Loud gravel. "My mom left the windows open. Crickets are sooooo noisy. Did you look outside?"

I clutched the phone tight. "Just out back. Why?"

"Check your front yard."

I sprinted to the living room window feeling nervous again.

A line of kids stood waiting outside my front door. The line was growing longer and twistier by the second.

I recognized most of the kids, but some weren't from the cul-de-sac. They wore Poplar Prep polo shirts in Easter egg colors. There were so many they spilled onto Peter's lawn.

"Eeek!" I squealed into the phone. I'm pretty sure it was the first squeal of my life.

"I know!" Clover squealed back. "I'll be right over."

I got dressed as fast as humanly possible. But on my way downstairs, I slowed down. I was Gilda

Stones. *Dr.* Gilda Stones. Dr. Gilda Stones was in charge.

I opened the front door.

The polo brigade came at me from all sides. Hot, bubblegum-scented breath filled the air, choking me.

I slammed the door shut.

"Space, people! Give her space!" I heard Clover yell. "Dr. Stones, it's okay. You can come out."

I opened the door again.

The crowd parted. Clover stood in the middle, still dressed in her cat PJs.

Polo-shirted kids on either side of me shoved their fancy phones in my face.

I grabbed Clover's pajama sleeve. She stepped in front of the cameras, waving kids off with a stack of frozen waffles. "No pictures!" she said.

"That's Gilda Stones?" a girl in blonde Elsa braids asked. "*The* Gilda Stones?"

"She looks different in person," her friend with reverse French braids replied. "Tinier."

"Where did they come from?" I whispered to Clover.

She shrugged. "Mel's review. You went viral."

I gulped. My eight little pyrite nuggets didn't stand a chance.

The line grew longer. New kids kept showing up. And the ones who'd already had a turn went right back to the end of the line.

If Clover hadn't painted my nails with 24 Karat Gal polish, I would have chewed them right off. El Dorado had a serious problem. My demand (people wanting pyrite) was greater than my supply (amount of pyrite). That's what Janet March calls "a good problem." It means you're successful. But it also means people get mad at you, so a good problem is still a problem.

Glitter, grass, and dirt covered the truth—there was no pyrite left in my panning stream. And I was the only one who knew it.

A little girl I didn't know stepped up to pan, probably a kindergartner. Her pink polo matched her pink glitter sneakers. She grinned up at me, showing three missing teeth, and held up a crisp five-dollar bill.

"Ith from the tooth fairy," she said.

I stared at her tooth gaps. They were all I could see. The money, the panning stream, the polo shirts—everything else went out of focus.

It would be so easy to lie.

I could make money all day if I wanted—hand out pans with a smile and say "Good luck!" and "Maybe next time!" when customers struck out.

After all, I wasn't selling pyrite. I was selling a game, like the claw machine at the Cone Zone. It let people down all the time. You put in a dollar and watched the claw hover for a while. Then it dropped and tried to pick up a stuffed animal or some other toy. Most of the time, the claw didn't catch anything at all. And it didn't say nice things to make you feel better.

But I wasn't a claw machine. I was a human.

I would tell my customers the truth. Not just because it was the right thing to do, but because I had to make up for liars like Peter. I wanted to prove you don't have to lie or cheat to succeed.

The kindergartner stood waiting, her tooth fairy money in hand.

"I'm sorry, everyone," I announced. "El Dorado is out of pyrite for now."

The crowd groaned.

"Waaaaahhhh," cried the kindergartner.

"No way!" shouted a squeaky voice near the back.

"Unacceptable!" yelled a boy whose voice was changing.

I had about three seconds to spin the situation. That's what Janet March calls it when you make something bad seem good.

"Um," I said. I cleared my throat. "Pyrite is exclusive. It's valuable and special. If there was a lot of it, um, you wouldn't want it, right?"

All at once, kids lowered their heads and tapped on their phones.

"What are they doing?" I whispered to Clover.

"Probably leaving bad You Reviews on Mel Chang's blog," she said with a sigh.

"But I told them the truth," I said.

Clover shrugged. "Maybe you should've lied."

mel chang's YOU REVIEWS!

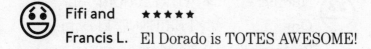

😃 **Fifi and** ★★★★★
Francis L. El Dorado is TOTES AWESOME!

😁 **Tanner Q.** ★★★★ Cool place. The fight to be first in line was good, too— because I won.

😑 **Ethan C.** ★★★ I didn't get to pan. They ran out of pyrite. Bummer. Dr. Gilda Stones better get it together tomorrow. Oh, and Team Tanner!

😊 **Mike the Unusual Magician** ★★★ Check out my first comedy/magic show next weekend at Clover O'Reilly's birthday party. Bring an appetite for amazement.

Nora P. ★★

They ran out of pyrite, but it's still better than the rock store next door. That guy is way too pushy.

 Number One Professional

★ WHAT A HORRIBLE EXPERIENCE. El Dorado is an amateur operation run by an amateur. First, Dr. Gilda Stones isn't even a real doctor. Second, glitter is a health hazard. The city should shut this operation down. But the place next door (Rocks Rock!) is a winner. *That* is how you run a business. Peter Gronkowski (I believe that's the gentleman's name?) is a bona fide success. Highly recommended.

19
PETER

Sunday. 7:57 a.m.

A long line of kids stretched across my lawn, spilling onto Rachel's. Most of them wore Poplar Prep polo shirts.

Finally. My empire was spreading.

Take it. It's yours. Tom Reddi's brilliant words echoed in my head.

This wasn't just about my family. This was about my future. Going to B school. Moving into Fountain's Spout Landing. Financing adult braces. My brand. My legacy.

This was about me.

"Hello!" I said to the crowd. "Welcome to Peter Presents: Rocks Rock! My intern Daniel will make you comfortable. But you're facing the wrong way. That's my house." I pointed behind me.

They turned around. My house didn't look like rich people lived there. The paint was peeling, and one of the gutters was falling off. These kids were used to pools. Circular driveways. Lawn services. All we had was a broken sprinkler that squirted sideways.

"Huh?" a boy with spiky hair asked. "What's Peter Presents? Who are you?"

I slapped him on the back. "Hoo-hoo-ha," I said. "Good one."

He frowned.

"I thought this was the line for El Dorado (A 4-D Interactive Experience)," said a tall girl in a yellow polo.

"Me, too," her short friend said. She sounded like a mouse.

Up ahead, I saw Jose and Roderick, Ken's Poplar Prep buddies. They were facing Rachel's house, too.

 BUSINESS TIP: Every challenge is an opportunity.

"Well," I said loudly, not yelling. "If you'll excuse me, I need to take care of a pressing matter. In my office. With my intern." I grabbed Daniel's hand and walked up to my house.

"Where are we going, Peter?" he asked.

 BUSINESS TIP: Walk, don't run.
Even when you want to get out of
somewhere as fast as possible.
Running shows desperation.

I closed the front door behind me, not slamming it.
This isn't happening. This isn't happening. This isn't happening.

This was happening.

They weren't here for me. They were here for Rachel Chambers.

 Business tip: There are no challenges.
Only opportunities.

I fluttered my eyelids. I Visualized the crowd of people waiting outside. They were there to see me. They just didn't know it yet.

"Daniel," I said. "Please load my trophies into the Peter Presents, Inc., Mobile Workplace."

"On it, boss!" Daniel said.

When those kids saw I was a real professional with employees and professional awards, they'd know I meant business.

We went back outside. The jackhammers at Ken's house had started up, so the crowd was even louder than before. I put on my headset and paced in extra-large circles on my lawn. Where was Ken, anyway? At least he wasn't in line.

"Why yes, Mr. Reddi," I said forcefully, not shouting. "*Twenty* orders? I'll get my intern right on it."

They didn't hear me. They were fighting to get to the front of the line.

 BUSINESS TIP: Yelling is unprofessional. But it's allowed in emergency situations when no one is listening to you.

"THIRTY ORDERS?" I yelled into my mouth-piece. "NO PROBLEM. PETER PRESENTS, INC., IS ALL ABOUT CUSTOMER SERVICE."

Just then, Rachel's door opened. The kids swarmed into her house.

The whole cul-de-sac went quiet, even the jackhammers. I was all alone. Almost.

"Peter?" Daniel asked. He was twirling one of my trophies like a baton.

 BUSINESS TIP: Use what you've got.

What I had was a four-year-old intern who liked dancing. In public.

"Daniel, you know the Saucy Subs guy?" I asked him. The Saucy Subs guy stands at the roundabout in downtown Poplar. He spins a Saucy Subs sign and dances and does the splits. I admire his dedication to building buzz.

"Uh-huh," Daniel said.

"Do you want to be like him?"

"Uh-huh!" he said louder.

"Good," I said. I took the ROCKS ROCK! sign down from its high spot. "I want you to spin this sign just like him. And show off your break-dancing moves."

"*Yes!*" Daniel shouted.

He spun the sign and threw it in the air. It landed on his face.

I turned his leprechaun hat upside down for tips. That wasn't in my original business model, but every minute that passed meant another minute I wasn't making money.

While Daniel showed off his Level 1 YMCA break-dancing moves, I slipped on my headset.

 BUSINESS TIP: Act as though everything is going according to plan.

After a few minutes, a flood of kids poured out of Rachel's house. They were grumbling.

"Spin, Daniel," I said. "And dance. Dance for your life."

"Dance for your life" is a one-on-one dance battle they teach at the Y. One kid does a move, then points to another kid to do a different, harder move.

Daniel got down on the grass and spun on his back. He pointed at me. I snapped my fingers and tapped my foot.

Just then Jose and Roderick walked over.

"Hey, guys," I said, tapping my foot harder like it was something professionals did on purpose. "What's going on?"

"Not much," Jose said. "We just texted Ken to hang out. Can we chill here?"

"There's no loitering," I said, "but I can make an exception."

"Hey, what's on your face?" Roderick asked.

My rash cream. I thought I'd blended it in.

"It's for zits," I said.

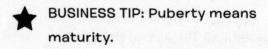 BUSINESS TIP: Puberty means maturity.

"Oh," Roderick said. "So you sell rocks, huh?"

"That's right," I said. "The highest quality ground merchandise."

"We were at El Dorado next door," Jose said. "But Dr. Stones ran out of pyrite."

I snorted. "How unprofessional," I said. Rachel couldn't handle basic supply and demand? What an amateur.

"She said she'll have more tomorrow," Roderick added.

"Sounds like an empty promise to me, gentlemen."

Roderick shrugged. We watched in silence as Daniel tried to spin on his head.

Ken jogged over from his house.

"Peter!" Ken said. "Man, I heard you were sick yesterday. Is it true you had a heart attack?"

"No," I said. "I'm eleven." That was one problem with living in a cul-de-sac. Rumors. Business professionals don't get sick. Illness is weakness.

Ken hadn't been over for Friday night dinner in two weeks. His hair looked different. It was spiky like Jose's. It made him seem taller.

"Hey, do you do friend discounts on rocks?" Jose

asked me. He held up #43: Gorgeous Granite. "I dig this one."

Rich people. They always want free stuff.

That gave me a brilliant idea.

Problem: I needed money to buy Rachel out.

Solution: Engage rich business investors. Entice them with free cupcakes.

"Ken, let's sidebar," I said, guiding him away from the booth.

"What's sidebar?" Ken asked when we were out of earshot.

"Look," I said. My head dripped sweat like a Fountain's Spout water feature. "I need you to follow Rachel Chambers."

Ken paused. "Why?"

"To find out where she gets her pyrite."

Ken scratched his wrist. "That's creepy," he said.

"It's not creepy. It's market research," I said. "If you're scared, you don't have to do it." Since Ken is a former/sometimes current scaredy-cat, I knew that would get his attention.

Ken glared and stood up straight. "I'm not scared!" he replied.

"Good." I checked my watch. "Be back for an emergency meeting in my garage at five p.m. Tell

Jose and Roderick to come. We'll make it a happy hour thing. With cupcakes. They're free."

"What do you mean, a happy hour thing?" Ken asked. He crossed his arms. "Is that fun? Or business?"

"Both," I said. "I have a fun business opportunity for them. Don't forget to mention the free cupcakes."

Ken paused. "Okay." He shoved his hands in the pockets of his full-price Abercrombie & Fitch jeans. "Maybe we can all hang out at my house afterward. Watch some Scare TV. Or we can teach you chess."

"Maybe," I said.

I calculated the profit and loss of hanging out in my head. The profit was seeing Ken and deepening business connections with Fountain's Spouters. The loss was time spent away from the business, which meant letting Rachel win, which meant no money, which meant losing everything.

 BUSINESS TIP: Success takes sacrifice.

———•———

5:00 p.m.

Ken was still out on his market research mission. I had to start the emergency meeting without him.

"Thank you all for coming today," I said to Jose and Roderick. My voice echoed in the garage. "I have an exciting business opportunity I can't wait to share with you. Go ahead and dive into the cupcakes. Did I mention they're free?"

Dad must have missed the key takeaway of the "Laid Off but Not Lying Down" article. I had to wake him up from a couch nap to make the cupcakes. I didn't know he was asleep at first because there were tea bags on his eyelids.

Jose looked like he really did dive into them. His shirt and face were covered in strawberry frosting.

Roderick messed around on his brand-new Winter White EtherPhone watch. Technically my watch was worth more because it was made of gold. Gold is classic. It appreciates in value.

The side door creaked open. Ken ran inside, red and sweaty. He gave me a thumbs-up. I nodded.

"Sorry I'm late," Ken said. "That, uh, took a while."

"No worries," I said. That phrase is not in my personal vocabulary. I was just mirroring Jose because I'd heard him say it before.

I cleared my throat. "Has anyone ever heard of an angel investor?"

BUSINESS TIP: Ask smart questions, even if you're 100 percent sure people won't know the answer.

Jose shook his head. Ken shrugged. Roderick looked up from his watch and nodded.

"Wait," I said. "You really know what an angel investor is?"

"Sure," said Roderick. "An angel investor gives you money for your business. It's someone who believes in you and your product."

"That's . . . right," I said. "How did you know that?"

"I backed my little sister's perfume stand last year. Diva Scents."

 BUSINESS TIP: Don't roll your eyes at potential investors, even if they've made terrible investments in the past.

I cleared my throat. "I'm offering you the opportunity to be angel investors in Peter Presents, Inc."

I paused for applause or excited mumbling. Roderick raised his hand. I nodded.

"Angel investors get something in return for their money, right?" Roderick asked.

I raised an eyebrow. "I'm glad you asked." I was not glad he asked. I didn't like the direction this meeting was taking. "My intern will hand out a worksheet showing the benefits of becoming an angel investor in Peter Presents, Inc. You'll have the satisfaction of getting in on the ground floor of a growing start-up. Daniel?"

Daniel stood up and handed out my fliers. I pretended not to notice that he was wearing boxer briefs as shorts.

"Thank you, Daniel," I said. "You're excused."

He took a bow and ran upstairs.

Roderick raised his hand. I clenched my teeth.

"What's your vision for the company?" he asked.

I relaxed. "My vision is that I want to be the most successful businessman in the history of the world," I said. That was easy.

"Okay," said Roderick. "Can I see your financials?"

"My financials?"

"Profit and loss statements, projections, that kind of thing."

I raised an eyebrow at Ken. He shrugged. Who was this guy? He didn't seem like an angel to me. More like the opposite.

"I don't have that information at this time," I said slowly.

"Would we share the profits?" asked Roderick.

I stared him down. "The money has to go into the business."

"For what?" Jose asked through bites of cupcake.

"Business development," I said.

"Like buying rocks?" Jose pressed.

"No," I said. "I don't buy rocks."

"Then what are you buying?"

"It's a high-level executive matter," I said. "You wouldn't understand."

Jose raised his hand. This was turning into a very unhappy happy hour.

"If I give you money, will you change the name of your company to Jose Presents?"

"Hey," said Roderick. "What about Roderick Presents?"

"I know," Jose said. "What about Jose and Roderick Presents?"

"With two people, it's *present*. Jose and Roderick *present*, not *presents*!" said Roderick. "And why does your name come first?"

"Gentlemen!" I called. "This meeting is losing

focus. Angel investors are more behind the scenes . . . helpers. Their names aren't anywhere in the business." *Not my business,* I thought.

"Yeah, sorry," Roderick said, standing up. "I'm not ready to make an investment right now."

"It's a no for me, too," said Jose.

No. No?! I was so shocked I couldn't find the strength to answer their objections.

 BUSINESS TIP: Regain control of every situation.

"Thank you, gentlemen, but I don't think this is going to work out," I said loudly.

"Whatever," said Jose. "Ken, are we still doing monster movies at your house tonight?"

Ken nodded. Jose and Roderick walked out. Since when did they watch monster movies?

"Your friends don't know anything about business," I said after they left.

Ken stared at the floor.

"What did you find out about Rachel?" I asked him.

"Yeah." he said. He didn't look up. "Sorry, man. I lost her. She covered her tracks pretty well."

"Too bad," I said. "But we can still move forward."

I cleared my throat. Borrowing money from your rich best friend is a low-status move, but I had no choice. I had no one else to ask. "I need capital."

"What's that?"

"Money." My face burned. "We'll have a formal contract, of course. It's a terrific investment for you. Not charity."

Saying the word "charity" made my stomach feel tight.

"For what?" he asked.

"To buy Rachel out."

"What do you mean, buy her out?" Ken asked.

"It's called a hostile takeover," I said. "When I find out where she gets her pyrite, I'll buy the whole supply. Then she can't stay in business anymore."

"Isn't that cheating?"

"No," I said. "Pyrite is a commodity on the open market. If I can afford it, why shouldn't I buy it?"

"Yeah, I get that," Ken said. "It just seems . . . wrong."

"All's fair in love and war and business," I said. *I should write that down,* I thought. "Whose side are you on, anyway?"

"Yours, I guess. It just seems, I don't know. Shady."

"Shady?" I said. "Rachel Chambers is the shady

one. She started a secret business. She threatened me with lemonade. And carrots. She endangered my health."

"I don't know," he said. "She's not *really* hurting anybody."

"She's hurting my family," I said. "And my brand. My brand is me."

"But I'm saving my money for other stuff," Ken said.

"What stuff?" I asked. "Your house has eight point five bathrooms. Your parents will buy you anything."

Ken's ears looked like they were on fire. "I get an allowance."

"You have a maid."

"I got a laundry basket for my last birthday!" Ken said. "I feed the dogs and walk them. And I take out the trash." He paused. "I save money to buy special stuff. Like a scooter."

"A Lazer Edge razor scooter?" I said. "So you can ride to the Cone Zone with your new friends?"

"I don't know," Ken said, sticking out his chin. "Maybe."

"Maybe?" I said. I felt a little dizzy. Ken was supposed to be nice. He wasn't supposed to say that.

"Do you think they're better than me?"

"You don't want to hang out with me, anyway!" he shot back. "All you want to do is make money. You don't even want me at your house anymore."

"I have to make a living," I said. I was losing grip on my professional control. "Why do you still live here, anyway? Building on your house like that is selfish. It messes with everyone else's property values. Why don't you just move to Fountain's Spout with all the other rich people?"

"My dad says people are nicer over here," Ken said. He looked down. "I don't know if that's true."

"Fine!" I said. "Then go to your rich friends. I don't need you or your money!"

Ken looked up. For a second I thought he might cry because his face crumpled. I almost said I was sorry.

But then he glared. He stormed out and slammed the door behind him.

A sharp pain zigzagged through my chest. I wondered if I really was having a heart attack.

One, two, three. Granddad always said to count seconds in silence to calm down.

But this silence was too quiet. My best friend was

building his own Inner Circle. And I wasn't in it.

The pain started to come back. But then I heard a voice deep inside my brain. It wasn't Granddad. It was Tom Reddi:

Professionals turn pain into profit.

My Inner Circle was gone. I had no one but myself.

I didn't need Ken. I had everything I needed right here. I'd make my own life Smorgasbord.

I took all the money from my investment jars and moved it into a brand-new fund, the only one that mattered: Peter's Empire.

I was Coke. Rachel Chambers wasn't even Pepsi. She was the half-empty liter of Cool Mountain Cola going flat in my refrigerator. A knockoff. A copycat. An amateur. So was everyone else.

 BUSINESS TIP: Be your own boss.

20

Rachel

"When is payday?" Clover asked as she wiped up a glittery puddle. "I need money to make my birthday party super awesome."

"Oh," I said. I pretended to organize a stack of pans. "I kind of need more time."

Clover stopped wiping. "But you made thirty dollars today," she said. "I get fifteen. You said we'd split it, remember?"

"Yeah. But I have to buy more pyrite. All the money still has to go back into the business."

"So when are *we* going to make money?"

"Clover," I said. "I need you to be a team player. Trust me. I'm working on it."

Clover wrinkled her nose. "Ew. Don't be greedy like Peter, Gilda."

"It's Dr. Stones," I said. "And I am not like Peter."

We cleaned up the rest of the panning mess in silence.

Clover was kind of right. But the truth is, I'd done stuff for her my whole life and never asked for a penny. I'd written her speeches, helped her memorize lines, tutored her for spelling tests, even buttoned her jeans in the bathroom when she sprained her pointer finger.

What was work, and what was helping out a friend? Janet March said you shouldn't mix business with friendship. Now I understood why.

———•———

Later that day, I headed to the Children's Museum for more pyrite.

The oak trees dripped leaves into my path. *Crunch, crunch, crunch.*

Rustle.

That was no crunch.

I spun around. No one was there. Not even a squirrel.

You're paranoid, I told myself.

Still, I cut through the Poplar Park playground to throw off my maybe-imaginary follower. Paranoid or not, I had thirty dollars in my turtle change purse and a competitive advantage. No one, not even Clover, knew where I bought my pyrite.

Rustle.

My stomach did a backflip.

"Peter," I whispered. "Is that you?"

"Jolly ho," said an unnaturally deep voice with an English accent. "Nothing to see here."

I clutched my change purse. "I know it's you," I said.

Ken Spumoni stepped out from behind a jasmine bush. "It's not Peter," he said in his normal voice. "It's me."

I stepped back. "What are you doing here?" I asked.

"Just exploring the park," Ken said. He pointed to a wilted purple flower on the ground beside him. "Nice, uh, flora this time of year."

"Really?" I asked.

He shifted from one foot to the other. "No," he said. "I'm supposed to follow you."

"Let me guess," I said. "*He* put you up to this."

Ken nodded.

"Why?" I asked. Not that Ken would tell me the truth. He was Peter's best friend.

"He doesn't like to lose," Ken said. "Look, he's

been acting weird ever since . . . I don't know."

I was not interested in a Peter Gronkowski history lesson. "But why are you following me?" I asked.

"To find out where you get your pyrite. Peter said it was market research."

I rolled my eyes. "Do you mean spying?" I said.

Ken shrugged.

"Do you do everything Peter tells you to do?" I asked. "You don't have to, you know."

He shrugged again and picked dirt out of his thumbnail.

I knew what it was like to have that kind of best friend. You felt like you had to do everything they said. It wasn't easy to say no.

Ken looked up. "I won't follow you anymore," he said. "Just don't tell Peter."

"Don't tell him you didn't follow me?" I asked.

"Yeah," he said.

"Okay." And with that he ran off toward the cul-de-sac.

I walked backward the rest of the way to the Children's Museum, just to make sure. But Ken kept his word.

Maybe he wasn't a Peter-bot after all.

21
PETER

With so-called best friends like Ken Spumoni, who needed enemies? Or angel investors?

If my own cul-de-sac didn't appreciate me, I'd go somewhere else.

———o———

7:48 a.m., Monday.

Daniel and I took our talents to the Poplar Children's Museum. Daniel set up my trophies front and center in the Peter Presents, Inc., Mobile Workplace. At least it wasn't too high for him to reach.

"Rocks for sale!" Daniel shouted to the empty parking lot.

"Save it," I said. "They don't open for twelve minutes."

The museum was a brilliant choice for our newest Rocks Rock! location. First, rocks were educational. Second, school was closed. Parents who do educational stuff take their kids there. Third, a change of scenery is like a breath of fresh air. That's what Tom Reddi says every time he moves business locations.

7:53 a.m. A Totally Teal 2006 Ford Explorer pulled into the parking lot. My business instincts told me this was a family of four, average household income but ready to spend on the right product, and a likely soft spot for a four-year-old break-dancing leprechaun.

The mom and dad got out the car. The dad unfolded a giant double stroller. A family of four. My business instincts were right on.

"Bring your wow game," I told Daniel. "Show off your best moves."

The family made a circle around Daniel and cheered him on. The twins in the stroller clapped. The mom even threw a one dollar tip in his leprechaun hat.

"Glad you all enjoyed the show," I said. "Now, what kind of rocks are you in the market for today?"

"Aw, yeah," said a voice over the loudspeaker. "The Poplar Children's Museum is open for business! Friends and family, come on in!"

Way to ruin my sales pitch.

"Bye, cutie!" the mom said to Daniel as she rolled the double stroller up to the entrance. What was I, invisible?

Two kids from my school came over. They watched Daniel dance, but then their parents made them go into the museum.

8:24 a.m. Time to make a solid impression.

"Yes, Mr. Reddi, hello," I said into my headset. "How many orders today? Seventy? I'm sorry, seventy-five? Consider it done."

"Hi! Excuse me!" said a woman coming out of the museum. Her name tag said POLLY B., MUSEUM MANAGER.

"I'm on a call," I mouthed, holding up a finger.

She smiled but didn't move.

"Okay, Mr. Reddi. Mr. *Tom* Reddi," I said for Polly B., Museum Manager's benefit. "Terrific. We'll get that going. Have a good one. See you on the range." I pressed my hang-up button. "What can I do for you?"

"Peter, right?" she asked. "I'm Mrs. Buckleworth.

I know your mom from Zumba. Your dad's in my book club. I've heard so much about you!"

I watched potential customers pass me by. This was no time for small talk. "What can I do for you?" I asked again.

"Well, I'm the manager here at the museum. I have some bad news." Mrs. Buckleworth sighed. "I'm afraid you can't do this." She gestured at my booth.

"I have a business license," I said.

 BUSINESS TIP: Make your own business licenses. It saves money and time.

I always carry a pack of pre-printed licenses. They're signed by my mom. Well, I signed them for her. It's more efficient that way. I've seen her signature enough times on my tests to know what it looks like.

Mrs. Buckleworth studied my license. "I'm sorry, sweetie. I love your passion, and the booth is so cute. But I can't."

Sweetie? Cute? If I were a wild animal, my hackles would have gone straight up. Did people go into the museum and call her job cute? How offensive.

"You can't?" I repeated. "You can't what?"

BUSINESS TIP: When someone says something you don't like, repeat it back to them. They'll realize they sound ridiculous, and you'll get your way.

"For one thing, I can't have you blocking the entrance," she said. "That's a fire hazard."

"We're a mobile business," I said. "My intern will move us to the parking lot. Now, where were we? You look like a limestone kind of gal."

Mrs. Buckleworth paused. "Peter, we sell rocks in the gift shop. I'm very sorry, but you can't sell rocks here, period. It's a conflict of interest. A conflict of interest is—"

"I know what a conflict of interest is," I said, raising an eyebrow.

"I thought you might," she said with a smile. "You understand."

That was my line. People didn't use it on me. I had one last trick in my pocket.

"How does thirty percent of my profits sound?" I asked.

 BUSINESS TIP: Bribery will get you everywhere.

Mrs. Buckleworth shook her head. "I wish I could, Peter," she said. "But it's a no." She turned to walk back inside.

"I'm an American citizen!" I said. "You'll be hearing from my attorney, Diana Sharpe-Gronkowski, about this." I didn't want to play dirty. But she'd left me no choice.

Mrs. Buckleworth turned back. She didn't look mad. She looked like Daniel when Dad tickled his feet. Amused. Like I was some kind of entertainment. A break-dancing leprechaun's sidekick. A kid.

"Say hi to your parents for me, Peter."

I gritted my teeth as she walked back into the museum.

Conflict of interest? What kind of inferior rocks were they selling, anyway?

"Daniel," I said. "Watch the booth for forty-five seconds. Don't give anything away."

Just as I suspected, the gift shop was an amateur operation. All the rocks were shoved in a corner called "The Super Stones Collection."

I ran my finger along the labels. Granite, Limestone, Pyrite, Shale, Slate . . .

Pyrite.

Bingo.

My head dripped with sweat.

———•———

I was *this* close to launching my very first hostile takeover. I just needed enough money to buy every piece of pyrite in the gift shop. El Dorado would be finished. Tom Reddi would be proud.

I didn't have much in the Peter's Empire fund. Since I couldn't count on angel investors or "friends," I had to make money the old-fashioned way. I'd sell everything I owned.

My most valuable possessions included an autographed first edition Peter Presents, Inc., map of Poplar Lane, a stack of mint condition *Mind Your Business* issues, and a remote control pickle Ken got me for my birthday. I didn't want it around anymore.

I wheeled everything to the one place I knew I'd get a good value: the pawn shop.

———•———

Harlan's Cash-4-Gold Pawn Shop stood right next door to the Reddi Mart.

I lugged my wagon up the wobbly wooden steps

and peeked in the shop's dusty windows. No Chamber of Commerce awards. No trophies. No framed MBA from any B school.

Creak.

"Greetings, my good man," said a deep voice at the end of the porch.

I flinched.

Harlan glided back and forth on a swing. *Snip. Ping.* He was clipping his fingernails into an empty soda can. Most of them bounced off the edge.

"Greetings," I said. It seemed smart to start the relationship by mirroring Harlan's language. But I didn't want anything in common with Harlan.

Harlan and Tom Reddi are nothing alike. First, Tom Reddi would not clip his fingernails in the workplace. Second, I don't even know Harlan's last name. That means he's not a bona fide success. Third, Harlan is not on the Poplar Chamber of Commerce. I bet he's never even attended a local networking event.

"I've got some top-notch items," I said. "They're going fast."

Harlan bowed and gestured to the door. "To my chambers."

Harlan's black skull T-shirt had holes in it, and his jeans were covered in paint. I bet Tom Reddi didn't even own jeans. If he did, he would wash them. And Tom Reddi would never have a ponytail.

Bells jangled when I pushed the door open.

Inside it smelled like the shoe rentals at the Cone Zone bowling alley. Guns and guitars hung on the walls. Jewelry sparkled in glass cases.

"What have we here?" Harlan asked, slipping on a pair of glasses.

First, he flipped through an issue of *Mind Your Business*. Tom Reddi's face was on the cover.

"That's the famous 'Pave Your Career Path with Gold' issue," I said.

Harlan snorted and held the magazine up to the light. "Tom Reddi, huh? He tried to boot me out of here a few years back. I didn't take the bait." He winked.

I winked back to mirror him, but obviously I was on Tom Reddi's side.

2:16 p.m. Harlan studied the map with a magnifying glass.

2:17 p.m. Harlan shined a flashlight at the pickle.

2:18 p.m. I tapped my finger on the handle of my wagon. Time is money. The Children's Museum closed in two hours and forty-two minutes. I also promised Mom I'd read the King Midas story today.

2:20 p.m. Harlan set the magnifying glass down.

"I can give you fifty cents for the funny pickle," he said.

Fifty cents. That was one eighth of a piece of pyrite.

"What else?" I asked.

"Nah," he said. "Nothing else."

"There must be some mistake," I said. "The map is a first edition. It's autographed. By me."

"What else you got for sale, son?" he asked.

I had nothing. Zero. My success was slipping away right before my eyes.

Then I did something that was not in any *Mind Your Business* I'd ever read.

"Man to man," I told Harlan. "Business owner to business owner. I need the money. Bad."

I tried to stare Harlan down but he wouldn't look me in the eye. He stared at my wrist. At Granddad Gronkowski's gold watch.

Harlan raised one furry eyebrow. "My good man," he said. "Everybody's got somethin' to sell."

22

Rachel

"Wait," I said to Carlos the gift shop cashier. "You're out of pyrite?"

"All gone," he said.

"But that's not possible!" I said. "You had a ton left yesterday. I was here. I saw it!"

"Some kid in a leather jacket cleaned me out earlier," Carlos said. "Parted hair. Sunglasses. What's with you kids and pyrite?"

I knew exactly one kid with parted hair and a leather jacket. And there was exactly one kid who would wear sunglasses indoors. Peter Gronkowski.

I leaned forward over the counter. "When do you get more pyrite?" I asked.

Carlos typed on his keyboard. "Next shipment comes a week from today."

Spring break would be over by then. It was too late.

The hare had won.

———•———

On the way home, I kicked every rock in my path. I even walked off the path to find more rocks to kick.

I imagined a world where Peter Gronkowski kept winning. It was like being led around by the Ghost of Christmas Future in *A Christmas Carol*.

"Good effort, Scoots," Dad would say. "When one door closes, another one opens! Did I mention we're having Chinese?"

"Woo-hoooooooo!" Clover would squeal. "I'm so glad you're over this business thing. Now you have all the time in the *world* to help me plan my party! Also, can you help me memorize my lines for the school play? I'm the star. It's called *Anastasia Emerald: The Musical*. Catchy, right? Oh, and make sure you finish up my campaign posters. And I'll need you to write my victory speech . . ."

I looked even further into the future. Peter was a grown man. He became the richest, meanest, most powerful boss in the world.

I was his unpaid maid.

"Business tip," Future Peter said, chomping on a cigar. His arms and legs took up so much space they blocked the sun. "Use an extra soft toothbrush on my premium gold watch collection. Only one hundred and fifty-two watches left to clean. Start scrubbing . . . what was your name again?" He cackled.

I got so lost in my nightmare I tripped over a cypress knee.

"Ow!" I yelled, rubbing my sore toe. Cypress knees stick up from the ground like they own the earth. They're always in the way and highly annoying . . . even dangerous. Just like Peter.

I stood up. This wasn't just about me. It was about every kid Peter Gronkowski had ever hurt and would ever hurt in the future.

A professional isn't a special person born to rule other people. A professional is just an amateur who didn't give up.

I won't give up.

Despite my throbbing toe, I sprinted home. I was out of pyrite, but I had hope—and a can of Midas All-Weather Spray Paint.

Peter Presents: P PYRITE!

Class. Quality. Luxury.

☀ ☆ ☀

From the established, professional brand that brought you Rocks Rock! comes . . . P Pyrite.

Why waste your time "panning" when you can get P Pyrite right away?

P Pyrite has zero glitter. Glitter has been proven to cause *dangerous allergic reactions.* P Pyrite is also both nut and gluten free.

P Pyrite. DRINK IT IN.

Go with the brand you know. The brand you trust. Not an unproven amateur who can't even keep product in stock.

Reliable. Satisfaction guaranteed.

P. One letter. It's all you need.

23
PETER

For the first time in forever, Dad picked up Chinese food.

"We saved enough in the Hog Wild fund this week!" Dad said as he folded a paper napkin in his lap.

"How?" I asked. I hadn't put anything in there since I was running Fabulous Fortunes.

"A little here, a little there," Dad said. "It adds up. Should we wait for Ken?"

"No," I said. I pushed away my plate. Suddenly I wasn't hungry.

"What's wrong?" Mom asked.

"I don't like Chinese food anymore."

Mom raised an eyebrow. "You feeling okay?"

"Terrific," I said.

After dinner I went to bed. I dreamed I led an executive board meeting with no pants on. That's how I felt without my watch.

Selling the watch to Harlan was a solid business decision. I shook his hand. The deal was done. And it was worth it. I'd completed my first hostile takeover. I had all the pyrite in Poplar. We were ordering take-out. And I didn't need Ken or anyone else to do it. I did it all by myself, just like Tom Reddi.

The next morning, I skimmed the "Hostile Take-over" issue of *Mind Your Business* for inspiration. It also featured one of Tom Reddi's finest editorials (or Redditorials, as he calls them), "How Do You Sleep at Night?" A regular editorial is where the editor tells you his or her opinion. But a Redditorial is a very special, intimate look into the mind of a genius.

Tom said amateur news reporters would jump out from behind bushes and surprise him with questions about his "unethical" business practices. That made him mad. So he started following the reporters and jumping out of bushes to surprise *them* instead.

"I always get the last laugh," wrote Tom.

Me too.

I headed downstairs for a Success Breakfast. My appetite was back, for food and for winning.

Daniel was already there when I walked into the kitchen. Slurping milk and cereal out of *my* bowl. My Daring Duckbill dark green, personalized Peter Presents, Inc., bowl.

Take it, I imagined Tom Reddi saying. *It's yours.*

"That's *mine*," I said, yanking my bowl out from under him.

"*No!*" Daniel yelled. He reached for the bowl, making milk slosh everywhere. It flew across the kitchen, hit the floor, and shattered.

"Peter!" Dad said. "Please clean that up."

"Daniel started it!" I said. "He stole my bowl!"

"It's nobody's bowl now," Dad said. His voice was low and serious. Almost professional. "Daniel, stay in your seat until Peter's done. I don't want you cutting up your bare feet."

I stuck out my chin and sopped up the mess with generic Tough-n-Thirsty paper towels.

"Grrr," Daniel said. "I have bear feet, Peter. Grrr."

I didn't crack a smile.

I knew Daniel wasn't my real enemy. But for some reason he (and everyone else) was starting to look like Rachel.

I ate my Success Breakfast out of a pathetic red plastic bowl. What an amateur way to start the day.

Later, Daniel the Bowl Destroyer and I went outside to set up.

Right away the smell of lemonade invaded my nostrils. There were four stands open already. One of them belonged to Daisy O'Reilly, Daniel's new wife.

"Daisy!" Daniel said. He waved. She waved back. He blew her a kiss across the street. She caught it on her mouth. Gross.

Daisy taped a sign on her booth: LEMONADE DIVAS.

 BUSINESS TIP, especially for lady entrepreneurs: Think beyond the word "diva." It's almost as bad as lemonade.

This was all Rachel Chambers's fault. She wasn't just bad for my business. She was bad for business, period. She gave amateurs false hope. She made them believe they could succeed, too. It was sad, really.

"P," said Daniel. He bent over laughing. "P!"

"What's so funny?" I asked, straightening the giant "P" sign in front of the booth.

"P!" he said, pointing to the sign.

"Congratulations. You can read a letter." I clapped slowly. "From preschool to B school."

"*Pee!*" Daniel yelled. "In the bathroom!"

"Knock it off," I hissed.

I did ten Deep Dive Lunges. I Visualized hordes of pyrite seekers.

When I opened my eyes, I saw a line forming outside Lemonade Divas.

I slipped on my headset and paced.

"Tom!" I said. "Hope I didn't catch you on the front nine."

Who cared about generic lemonade stands? Who ruled Amateur Alley? Me. The only pyrite provider in town.

Soon I'd be able to afford one hundred and twenty personalized cereal bowls. I'd hire fifteen extra-tall interns who could both read and write. They would put my bowls on the highest shelves in the world, where Daniel or Dad could never find them.

———•———

Time unknown. Mel Chang stomped up to my booth in her heavy black shoes.

"Mel Chang, my favorite Poplar Lane blogger," I said. "How about a glass of Rockin' Refresher?" Rockin' Refresher was the same thing as Truth Tonic from Fabulous Fortunes. I just threw some leaves in a jug of Gator Green sports drink and gave it a new brand name.

 BUSINESS TIP: Recycling your old ideas is the key to a successful operation.

Mel's hair swooshed as she shook her head. "No, thanks. I just want to see your pyrite."

"All business," I said. "I can appreciate that, Mel."

 BUSINESS TIP: Use a person's name over and over in a conversation. It makes them feel important.

I wiped my palms on my leather jacket before handing her my highest-grade luxury sample. She studied it like a detective.

"There's a P on it," Mel said.

"P is my brand, Mel," I said. "Like O for Oprah."

Mel wrinkled her nose and handed the pyrite back like it was poisonous. "I'm going to be very honest with you," she said.

"Please do, Mel." I stood up to my full height. She was still about two heads taller than me.

She pushed up her thick black glasses. "This isn't good."

"What isn't good?" I asked.

"Your brand," she said.

"P?"

"Peter," she said slowly. "What do you think of when you think of P?"

I rubbed my chin. "Peter. Peter Presents. Poplar Prep. Professionalism. Pyrite. Pot stickers."

"Do you know what I think of?" she asked.

"What?"

Mel lowered her voice. "Urine."

I winced.

"Exact," Mel said. "I don't want to feel gross about a product." She shook her head. "Your brand is not what it used to be, Peter."

I stared at her. I tried to speak, but my mouth wouldn't move.

"I can't promote something that makes me think of . . . bathrooms," she said. "I'd be the laughingstock of the cul-de-sac. Of Poplar Middle. The whole Internet." She paused. "You should really sell RC pyrite. The Rachel Chambers brand. That would be brill."

My nostrils flared like a dragon's. "I do not and will not ever sell RC pyrite, *Mel*," I said.

"But she's the original," Mel said. "You're selling a knockoff."

"I am not a knockoff," I said. "Rachel Chambers is

done." *It's the same pyrite!* I wanted to professionally scream.

Beep. Mel checked her phone. "My source says Rachel has something new and different. Something . . ." She squinted. "Innovative."

"Sorry. Your source is an idiot," I said, folding my arms across my chest.

"Look." She shoved her phone in my face. A purple message stretched across the screen: "EL DORADO IS BACK and BETTER THAN EVER! Pan for REAL GOLD with Rachel 'The Real Thing' Chambers."

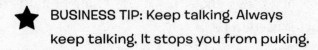

BUSINESS TIP: Keep talking. Always keep talking. It stops you from puking.

"Seriously, Mel," I said. "Where would a twelve-year-old get real gold? Hoo-hoo-ha!"

"I don't ask questions," Mel said. "I just give my readers the info they want. And they're going to want gold." She flexed her fingers. "You understand."

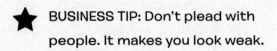

BUSINESS TIP: Don't plead with people. It makes you look weak.

"Please, Mel," I whispered.

"It's business, Peter. Not personal," Mel said with a shrug. "Rachel Chambers is hot, and you're not."

Tap, tap, tap. The sound of doom.

I sank into my Executive Lawn Chair. My brand, my name. They were both worthless.

I wasn't Peter Gronkowski of Peter Presents, Inc., king of the Poplar Lane cul-de-sac. I was Peter Gronkowski, the friendless amateur who sold a gold watch for pyrite.

24

Rachel

The can of Midas All-Weather Gold spray paint felt cold in my hand. So cold I had to put it down.

Clang. The metallic sound echoed through my garage.

I reached into my warm pocket. Inside was a dry rock from the El Dorado panning stream pile. I pulled it out and set it on some old newspaper.

Then I picked up the spray paint.

"Don't I look pretty, Rachel?" the can asked me. "Don't I look like real gold? No one will know the difference. All you have to do is spray paint this itty-bitty rock. No one will know. . . ."

Okay, the can of spray paint wasn't actually talking. But it was easier to imagine that than to admit that the idea came from my own brain . . . that I could lie like Peter.

But I wasn't like Peter. This was a lie for good, not evil. I wouldn't be stopping small business owners and crushing people's hopes and dreams. My lie would stop the evil Peter Gronkowski from taking over the cul-de-sac and the entire world.

The little mixing ball inside the can rattled around like dice when I shook it.

I pressed the nozzle over the rock. *Shhhh.*

The burst of paint came out fast. In less than a second, the boring gray rock was a golden nugget.

I looked from the nugget to my mom's ring. The nugget didn't look like pyrite. Pyrite was darker, and it sparkled.

But did the nugget look like real gold?

Other than Peter's watch, I'd never seen real gold before. But his watch was shiny and polished (thanks to me), not like gold you'd get from the ground.

I let the paint dry while I hid my supplies under a drop cloth.

Inside I searched "gold nuggets" on Dad's computer. I held the spray-painted rock up beside a picture of a real gold nugget.

I gasped. They were twins.

———————————

Later that night, Clover came over. I pulled her into the garage.

"What's in here?" Clover asked.

"Just . . . something," I said.

I had a plan—a plan to confess, even though I hadn't even done anything bad yet. I'd show Clover my pile of painted rocks, and she would stop me from making a horrible, lying decision.

"Mmmmm," Clover said. She closed her eyes and inhaled. "Paint smell." To an artist, "paint smell" is like exotic perfume.

I swallowed hard. I had my speech ready: *Do you know why it smells like paint? Because I'm a terrible person. I spray-painted a bunch of rocks to pretend they're real gold. Then I'm going to sell them. Do you think that's okay? Yeah, me neither.*

I took a deep breath. I opened my mouth.

"Oh. Em. Gee," Clover said, pointing to the pile of gold-painted rocks in the corner. "What is *that*?"

I closed my eyes and took another deep breath.

But the words that came out of my mouth didn't match the thoughts in my brain.

"Gold," I lied. "It's gold."

"GOLD?!?!!?!?!?!" Clover squealed. "Where did you get it?"

"Trade secret," I said. My smile felt weak, like it had the flu.

Clover frowned. "The hair salon in the mall?"

"No," I said.

Clover is gullible. That means "easily tricked." If you told her you adopted a pet unicorn, she'd wait on your porch with a glittery sign that said WELCOME HOME, UNIQUE! (her favorite unicorn name).

I didn't want to trick her. I didn't want to lie. But if I told her the truth, my business would fail. Peter Gronkowski would win. I'd go right back to being Puppet. A nothing. A nobody. Invisible.

"We have a big day tomorrow," I said, quickly changing the subject. "You're getting paid!"

Clover squealed.

"Awesome. Let's make new posters for the gold!" she said. "Oooh, I know. Get that gold spray paint I gave you."

"Oh!" I said. My voice sounded almost as loud as Clover's. "I think it's here somewhere."

I rummaged around even though I knew it was under the drop cloth.

"Found it!" I said. I held up the half-empty can.

Lying is like dominos. After the first one drops, it's all over.

Clover shook the can. She sprayed "El Dorado, City of REAL Gold" on a sheet of white poster board.

"Where should we say you got it?" she asked. "Since it's a trade secret."

"Yeah," I said. Not everyone was gullible like Clover. "Um, put 'Gold Certified by Financial Expert Janet March.'"

Clover blinked twice. "Uh, I need you to write that down."

My hands shook as I wrote on a scrap of paper. Not only was I lying *to* Clover, but I was making her lie *for* me.

After Clover finished the poster, she wiped her hand across her face.

"There's paint on your cheek," I told her.

"Oooooooooh!" Clover said. She checked her reflection in a broken mirror by the garage door. "It's like makeup. For your brand!"

The word "brand" has different meanings. One is a noun, like someone's product. The other meaning is a verb. It's what farmers sometimes do to cattle. They burn a brand, or symbol, onto an animal's skin.

I had branded my very best friend with a lie.

———•———

That night, I dreamed that Janet March visited me in a golden cloak.

"Rachel, you're not lying," she told me. "You're marketing! That's what businesspeople do. It's called being creative. And please feel free to use my name! All publicity is good publicity."

"Then why does it feel so bad?" I asked her. I was wearing the Cowardly Lion costume from *Wizard of Oz, Junior* with a turtle shell on my back.

Peter popped up in bunny ears.

"You'll get used to it," he said, chomping on a baby carrot. "Business tip: Don't second-guess yourself."

Janet March smiled. "Exact-a-mundo! So, are we still on for surfing? I'll bring the steak knives."

Huh? I sat up straight in my bed, covered in sweat.

Maybe Janet March was right about marketing. Like the Wily Wizard at the Children's Museum . . . his fortunes weren't real. Everyone knows they're fake. They're just for fun.

Was spray-painting rocks and calling them gold really that wrong? What about Peter buying all the pyrite at the Children's Museum? Which one of us was worse?

The next day, Clover came over early.

"Why are you so chipper?" I asked as she hummed and skipped down my front hallway.

"Why are you so moody?" Clover retorted. "Anyway, it's almost my birthday *and* it's payday! Why shouldn't I be chipper?"

I shrugged.

"I texted Mel about the gold. She said she'd send out the info in a jif. What does that mean? Anyway, we'll totally have ten thousand customers today." Clover's eyes sparkled like (real) pyrite.

I winced. Could I lie to ten thousand more people?

I heard a tiny buzz coming from outside—just a voice or two. Then a swarm. Then an attack of killer bees.

Clover opened the door, and I pasted on my biggest Gilda Stones smile.

"Welcome to El Dorado," I said. "The Lost City of Real Gold."

25
PETER

Mel Chang's tweet caused an amateur avalanche.

Lemonade stands were abandoned. Kids poured in from every direction. They carried pumpkin baskets, paper bags, backpacks, and shoeboxes to hold all the El Dorado gold they could carry.

"It's Halloween!" Daniel said. "I forgot!"

Before I could tell him it was March, he was off with the other kids. Traitor.

 BUSINESS TIP: Every challenge is an opportunity.

"Pyrite for sale, pyrite for sale!" I called, waving my arms.

My opportunities barreled right past me.

No one cared about pyrite anymore. Why would they? The "real thing" was right next door.

Marty Danish, the biggest defensive lineman in Poplar Pop Warner football, plowed right into me. I fell back hard on my lawn.

My chest hurt. I sat up on my elbows and tried to take a few deep breaths. I Visualized that I was not on the ground because I got knocked over. I chose to be there.

A second avalanche spilled out of Rachel's house.

"I'm rich!" yelled Scott MacGregor.

"I don't ever have to get a job!" screamed Gabby Jonas.

Susie Lorenzo turned a sharp corner past Gabby, tripping over my rib cage. A gold nugget flew out of her Hello Kitty Easter basket and knocked me on the head.

Hadn't I taken enough abuse today?

I picked up Susie's nugget. It was smooth and round, all one color. It wasn't pyrite. Pyrite glitters, and it has jagged edges.

But something wasn't right.

I've been a branding expert my whole life. Once Grandma and Grandpa Sharpe bought Daniel and me a Mickey Mouse doll to share. Daniel thought it was the best present ever. But the doll seemed weird to me. I checked the tag. In extremely tiny print, it said "Mitchell Mouse."

It was a fake. A knockoff. When I told Daniel, he cried. I got in trouble. My parents didn't want to hear that knockoffs were harmful to the Disney brand. They wanted to send me to my room without dinner.

I squeezed the nugget tight. Maybe it smacked me in the head for a reason.

I searched for pictures of real gold nuggets on Mom's computer. They looked pretty much like Rachel's, except for the RC logo. The logo was written in black pen, the kind with the really thin tip. The bottom of the "C" stretched to make a circle around the initials. It was the second most impressive logo I'd ever seen, besides the *Mind Your Business* header.

My fingers itched. I looked down. They were covered in tiny red dots.

I groaned. Not again. A business professional, allergic to gold? That was just wrong.

Wait. No way was I allergic to gold. My granddad's watch was gold. I'd worn it every day.

I searched "How to tell if something is real gold." I found an article about athletes biting gold medals at the Olympics. Real gold, the article said, will show teeth marks.

What a waste of good gold, I thought. But I had to know. I held my breath and bit the nugget.

"Bluuuuuuuh!" It tasted like poison. I ran to the bathroom and spit in the sink. My tongue started swelling.

"Mom!" I yelled.

———◦———

For the second time in one week, I sat on Dr. Spumoni's examining table.

"Bad day at the glitter factory, Peter?" Dr. Spumoni said. He slapped his knee like it was the funniest thing anyone had ever said. I didn't smile. I couldn't have even if I wanted to. My face felt like a bowling ball.

"He says he's allergic to gold," Mom said, handing the nugget to Dr. Spumoni. "I have no idea. He wears a gold watch and never had any problems before." She looked at my naked wrist. "Peter, where's your watch?"

"Being cleaned," I said. "I bit the nugget to see if it was real." But with my swollen tongue, it sounded more like "I bith the nugget to thee if ith wath real."

"Uh-huh," Dr. Spumoni said with a chuckle. He held the nugget up to the light. "Could have fooled me, *too*, Peter. This is high-quality *paint*."

"Payt?" I said.

"It's just a regular old rock," Dr. Spumoni explained. "Painted, spray-painted, something."

My mouth was too puffy to say anything back. I didn't care. I had proof. Doctor proof. Proof that Rachel "The Real Thing" Chambers was a fraud.

❈ CLOVER'S BIRTHDAY BASH ❈ RED CARPET GALA!

Lights . . . Camera . . . AWESOME!

Clover O'Reilly is ready for her close-up AND she's turning twelve. Can you handle it? I can't!!

WHO: Clover O'Reilly (duh)!

WHAT: 12th Birthday Party!

WHEN: April 1, 12 noon (yes, Clover's birthday is on April Fool's Day! That's no joke. Really, it's not a joke.)

WHERE: The Red Carpet (aka Clover O'Reilly's house. The theme is "red carpet.")

WHY: You only turn 12 once!

Show up in your finest Red Carpet outfit and prepare to have your picture taken with a STAR (Clover)! But not too fine, because it's Clover's birthday, and she should SHINE the BRIGHTEST.

Also featuring a comedy/magic show by Mike the Unusual!

Party sponsored by RC "The Real Thing" Gold.

26

Rachel

Spring break was over, and suddenly everyone at school knew my name. My real name.

"Rachel Chambers!" said Scott MacGregor. He held the door for Clover and me and put his hand up for a high five. I slapped it, even though I half expected him to pull it back at the last second.

"Ha-ha!" he'd say. "I don't high-five huge liars!"

When you're doing something wrong, you don't trust the good times. Every day feels like danger.

"Garrrrrhhh," Clover moaned.

"What's wrong?" I asked.

"My bookbag is soooooo heavy," she said. "I have to take Peter's books to his house again."

"What's wrong with him?" I asked.

"I don't know," Clover said. "Maybe he had another heart attack. His head was sweaty."

I swallowed hard. There was no way Peter really had a heart attack. Still, I felt guilty, like even his sweaty head was my fault.

"Oh," Clover added. "He said he was going to drop a bombshell at my party. I said bombs were *not* allowed. He'd better not do anything weird."

A bombshell?

———•———

Sunday, 8:00 a.m. Four hours till Clover's party.

The rest of the week had passed by in a blur. Peter came back to school, but he didn't network at lunch or by the bike racks after the last bell. He just went home.

I should have been happy, but I wasn't. That creepy danger-feeling followed me everywhere.

I sat up in bed and stretched my arms in front of me. A gold speck of paint shone on my left thumbnail. I shook my head. When I looked again, the speck was gone.

Maybe it was one of those floaty moving dots in your vision that disappears when you blink. Or maybe I was losing it. I went downstairs.

"Hey, Scoots," Dad said as I came into the living room. He was reading *Single Parenting Your Tweenager.*

I sat on the couch beside him and turned on the news.

"This just in," the news anchor said, touching her earpiece. "Olympic champion Buddy Coletti admits to taking performance-enhancing drugs. He will forfeit his three gold medals. Buddy has declined to speak to the press. Later, more on the corporate corruption trial rocking Poplar County, after the break."

Dad looked up from his book. "Pride always comes before the fall," he said.

I studied Buddy Coletti's face on the screen. He was biting his gold medal and smiling. Did he know his time was running out? Was it better to win a gold medal and lose it than to never win a gold medal at all? Would I have to give up my Pulitzer Prize?

"You know what?" I said.

"What?" Dad said.

"I'm tired of adults telling kids they're supposed to follow the rules when they don't follow them either," I said.

Dad started to say something. Then he stopped, like he'd changed his mind.

A red carpet stretched from the sidewalk up to Clover's front door. Mr. and Mrs. O'Reilly wore T-shirts and hats that said PAPARAZZI. They were snapping tons of pictures.

"Rachel!" Clover ran down the red carpet, almost tripping over her long, glittery gold dress. She looked me up and down and frowned. "You didn't dress up."

"Oh," I said. "I forgot. I've been kind of . . . preoccupied."

"Eeeee!" said Daisy O'Reilly, right behind Clover. "I want a picture with Rachel!"

"Me too!" said Gabby Jonas. "Rachel, I looooove your outfit." She had on black rain boots and a satchel alarm clock, just like I wore when I was Gilda Stones.

"So designive," said Susie Lorenzo.

Designive? I checked to make sure I was still wearing khaki shorts and a navy blue T-shirt.

"Uh, thanks," I said. I handed Clover a gift bag.

Clover doesn't wait to open presents. It's not her "thing." She peeked in the bag.

"Oooh," she said. "It's gold! *Your* gold!"

I smiled. I'd gotten so good at lying it didn't even feel like lying anymore.

"Come on," Clover said, grabbing my hand. "Everyone's here!"

The O'Reilly's living room was chaos. Little kids chased the O'Reilly's cats. Others waited in line at a face-painting station.

Mel Chang waved at me from the face-painting chair.

"Rach!" Mel said. "That outfit is amaze." She turned to the face-painter, Clover's older sister Violet. "I have a brill idea. Can you do the RC logo instead of a clover?"

"Hey," said Clover. "It's *my* birthday. Clovers only!"

"And *I'm* the artist," said Violet. Clover pouted.

Kids formed a circle as Violet drew a tiny RC logo on Mel's cheek.

"I want one, too!" said Daisy.

Clover wrinkled her nose.

I felt a tap on my shoulder. "Rachel Chambers!" It was Amber Sledge, an eighth grader.

"I just need a moment of your time," said Amber. "I have a unique opportunity for you to invest in my business." She kept looking up while she was talking, like she'd memorized lines for a play.

"Um, okay," I said.

"The cul-de-sac's first outdoor nail salon–slash–lemonade stand. It's called . . ." Amber paused dramatically. "Lemonade Hand-Stand Divas."

"Um, my assistant Clover will set up a meeting," I said.

"Arrrrrgh!" Clover said. "No business stuff at my birthday party."

More kids wanted to take a picture with me. They laughed at everything I said, even if it wasn't funny. Kids who ignored me, kids who called me Puppet . . . they were suddenly my friends.

Clover stood in the corner with her arms crossed.

"Hey!" yelled Scott MacGregor. "Peter Gronkowski is here! He's not dead!"

Peter and Daniel strolled into the living room.

Peter's sunglasses sat on top of his head. He wore a yellow-checked button-down shirt with a green sweater tied around his shoulders, with khakis and boat shoes. His hair was slick, and his part was especially deep.

He didn't look like he'd had a heart attack. He didn't even look like he had a stuffy nose.

Peter shook hands with everyone, both kids and adults. That's what Janet March calls "working the room." But when he got to Ken Spumoni, he walked right by him. Weird.

Then Peter came up to me.

"Rachel 'The Real Thing' Chambers," Peter said. He looked me in the eye so sharp and straight I was worried he'd slice my eyeballs. He stuck out his hand. "Or is it Dr. Gilda Stones? Congratulations on your success."

"Thanks?" I said. His hand felt cool and dry. Before I even knew what had happened, Peter moved on to Mike the Unusual.

Mike was sitting cross-legged in a corner under a sign that said THIS IS WHERE THE MAGIC HAPPENS. His eyes were closed and he was chanting.

Peter tapped Mike on the shoulder. Mike took off his headphones. Peter said something. Mike shrugged. Peter leaned in closer and handed him a folded sheet of paper. Mike put it in his pocket, and they shook hands.

What was that all about?

"Attention, everyone!" Clover yelled into a microphone even though she didn't need it. "As you all know, it's my birthday!" She paused. I clapped. Then everyone else clapped, too.

"It's time for Mike the Unusual's comedy-slash-magic act!" Clover said. "So seriously stop talking.

Without further ado, I present: Mike the Unusual!"

Loud music blasted out of nowhere. The song was about getting stronger and flying higher. Mike jogged out wearing a silky robe and boxing gloves. He pretended to box the air, then flung off his robe. His T-shirt underneath said AMUSING ILLUSIONS: THE #1 COMEDY-MAGIC PODCAST.

"Hello, and welcome to Clover O'Reilly's birthday party!" Mike said into the microphone. "I'm psyched to be here today. Welcome to my comedy-slash-magic extravaganza. I won't let you down, Clover."

Clover blushed through her clover face paint.

"Ladies and germinators," Mike said. "I'm Mike, and this is my mike." He pointed to the microphone. "His name is Mike Two. We just flew in from next door, and boy are our arms tired." Silence.

"Germinators! Ha!" said Gabby.

"Anywuzzle," Mike said. *Anywuzzle?* I thought. "Mike Two and I are gonna have to warm you all up with a joke."

"Yeah, what is this, the Arctic Circle?" Mike said in an old-timey voice. I guess it was his micro-phone's voice. "If so, save me from the polar bears, spear me a salmon, and slap it on a bagel!"

Silence. Mr. O'Reilly snorted.

Mike held the microphone under his arm. He clapped and nodded at the audience. "You're at about a three, people. I need you at a ten! Can I hear you say CLOOOOOO-VERRR!"

"CLOOOOO-VER!" the crowd chanted.

"Anywuzzle, I have a very special guest today." Mike pulled the folded sheet of paper out of his pocket. "You know him from his successful business empire, Peter Presents, Inc. Please welcome my magician's assistant: Peter Gronkowski!"

"Yay, Peter!" screamed Daniel.

Peter whispered something in Mike's ear.

"Correction," Mike said. "My magician's *associate*. Anywuzzle, Peter asked if he could use the mike. And I said, 'I will not be used!'"

"Ha!" said Mr. O'Reilly.

"Anywuzzle, he said he'll give it back soon. And we agreed that soon means five minutes, right, Peter?"

"Terrific!" said Peter. He swiped the microphone out of Mike's hands. "First, happy birthday to Clover. What a great girl, right?"

Clover smiled, stood up, and took a bow.

Peter scanned the crowd like an owl searching for a mouse.

His eyes landed on me.

"And look who we have here. It's a local celebrity. Rachel 'The Real Thing' Chambers!"

The crowd cheered. I stood frozen.

"Rachel struck gold in her own backyard," he said. "What awesome luck. Can you believe it?"

The crowd nodded.

"Well, I can't," Peter said.

"Huh?" Gabby asked.

"You're just jealous," yelled Scott. A bunch of other kids booed.

"Ugh," Clover said. "Peter, stop. I want cake."

Mike took the microphone back from Peter. "Time for some magic!" Mike said. He nodded at Peter. "This trick is called Pyrite"—Peter held up a piece of P Pyrite with one hand—"or Gold?" In his other hand, Peter held up one of my nuggets. That hand was wearing a glove.

My stomach dropped like I was on a roller coaster that I was *way* too short to ride.

Peter snatched the microphone back from Mike. "Illusions are a big part of magic," Peter said. "Pyrite is fake gold. Pyrite leaves a black streak on a ceramic plate. Mike, will you do the honors?"

"Hey, you're *my* assistant," Mike said, taking the microphone.

"Associate," Peter corrected him, taking it back.

Mike sighed. He scraped the pyrite across a white plate. He held the plate up for the audience.

"Voila," Mike said. "It's black."

"Now for the gold," Peter said, rubbing his hands. "Real gold leaves a gold mark."

I gulped.

Mike scratched my nugget on another white plate. He held it up.

Nothing.

"Strange," Peter said, turning the stone over in his hand. "It says RC on here. That's *supposed* to be real gold."

"Stop!" yelled Clover. "Stop trying to make Rachel look bad, Peter Gronkowski. I bet that's not even hers."

She grabbed a nugget from the gift bag I brought her and gave it to Mike. "This one is definitely Rachel's." She gave me a knowing look.

I stared at the floor.

"Take two," Mike said, holding the nugget over a new white plate.

Scratch.

A couple of kids gasped.

Scratch.

It was quiet.

"Isn't that odd?" Peter said.

Clover covered her ears. "Peter Gronkowski, stop!"

"Don't you people get it?" Peter said. "Rachel Chambers sold you fake gold. She's a fraud."

Clover jumped onstage and snatched the microphone from Peter's hands.

"Hey, watch the arm!" shrieked Mike in his microphone voice.

"That's it," Clover said. "No one calls my best friend a fraud. Especially not you, Peter Gronkowski. And especially not on my birthday!"

"Rachel," Peter said calmly. "It's your turn."

I opened my mouth. Clover opened her mouth, too. I stood up before she could say anything.

"I'm sorry," I told her.

Clover shook her head. She looked wavy through the tears welling up in my eyes.

"No," she said. "Why? Why are you sorry?"

Then I saw it. The exact moment my best friend realized I'd betrayed her.

"You . . . you . . . lied," Clover said. "To me."

"She lied to everyone!" Peter said.

"But you lied to *me*," Clover said. For once, she was so quiet I could hardly hear her.

"Welp, that's a wrap," Mike said. "Don't forget to grab an invisible business card on the way out."

I'm not sure what happened next. I left Clover's house. I must have, because the front door slammed behind me.

27
PETER

 BUSINESS TIP: Good things come to those who wait.

Last week was the longest silent period of my life. I deserved an award just for keeping my mouth shut about Rachel's fake gold. I Visualized the trophy inscription: POPLAR'S MOST PATIENT AND PROFESSIONAL YOUNG ENTREPRENEUR.

At dinner, Daniel told my parents every single detail about Clover's party.

"And then, I got my face painted!" Daniel said. He pointed to his cheek, but you couldn't see anything under a mask of red sauce. "And then, I chased Cloudy! Cloudy is a cat! And then, Peter did a magic trick!"

"Cool," Dad said. "What kind of trick?"

"More of an experiment," I said as I swirled my spaghetti.

"And then Rachel cried!" Daniel said.

I groaned. Daniel is obsessed with crying. I've tried to tell him that crying equals weakness, but he doesn't listen. Do you think Tom Reddi cries? No way.

Dad raised both eyebrows. "Rachel cried? Rachel Chambers? Why?"

"Let's change the subject," I said.

"And then, Rachel said she was sorry!" said Daniel. "And then she ran away!"

"Why was she sorry?" Dad asked. He put his fork down. "Did she really run away?"

"No," I said. "Anyway, how would I know? This conversation is boring."

"I don't think so," Dad said.

"Look," I said. "Crying and running away are not relevant details. The key takeaway is that I won."

"What did you win?" Mom asked. She blinked like she was just waking up. "Sorry, my brain is scrambled from the trial. I'm confused."

I put down my own fork. "Okay," I said slowly.

"Rachel Chambers started a business. She lied to people. I told everyone that she lied. Now everything is fine. I won."

"What did she lie about?" Mom asked.

"It's not a relevant detail," I said, "but she spray-painted rocks and said they were real gold."

Dad laughed. "That's pretty smart."

"Smart?" I said. "She's a liar. Do you support liars?"

"No," Dad said. "Hey. I'm on your side, Peter."

"Good, because I'm the winning side," I said. "Let's eat."

We all chewed in silence for a few seconds. Then Dad said, "Winning isn't everything."

"You're right," I said. "Winning isn't everything. It's the only thing."

"Where did you learn that?" Dad asked.

"Not from you," I mumbled.

"Excuse me?" Mom said. She was suddenly wide-awake. "Over the line, Peter."

"It's true," I said. "Dad doesn't care about winning. He just said so."

"What did you win by telling on Rachel?" Dad asked.

"I won being the most successful businessperson

in the cul-de-sac," I said. "Don't you want your son to be a success?"

"Not if your success hurts other people," Dad said.

Daniel's head whipped around like he was watching a ping-pong match. Mom wasn't even checking her phone.

"I didn't hurt anyone," I said. "Some people are strong, and some people are weak. The strong survive and succeed."

"Peter, what does success mean to you?" Dad asked.

"Having money," I said. "Not being a loser. Being the best."

"I don't agree," Dad said.

"Obviously," I replied.

"Peter!" Mom said. She was full-on dragon breathing now.

"No, Diana," Dad said, holding up a hand. "Get it out, Peter."

"Well . . . what do *you* know about success?" I said. The truth shot out of me like an exploding volcano. "You got laid off. You never even looked for a job after that. Now you bake cookies and plant flowers. You're the Class Mom. You're not a good mentor for me *or* Daniel. And," I went on, "Granddad Gronkow-ski would be ashamed of you. He was a real success."

Dad stared at his lap.

My stomach felt empty, like I just threw up. I didn't know you could make yourself sick.

Please don't cry, I begged him in my head. Making your dad cry wasn't just unprofessional. It was personal.

Then Daniel started crying. Not a whiny baby cry. A real, sad cry. My whole body felt hollow.

"Peter, go to your room," Mom said quietly.

For once, I didn't negotiate. I deserved it.

———•———

I stared at the autographed picture of Tom Reddi on my bedroom wall. It came free with every purchase of a *Mind Your Business* subscription.

I licked my finger and ran it over his signature. It didn't smear. That meant it was printed by a computer, even though it was stamped "Guaranteed Authentic!"

Did that make Tom Reddi a bad person? He was a good businessman, obviously. Having computers sign your name is an efficient practice for any busy professional. But was it lying?

Was Tom Reddi a good person? Had he ever helped anyone? Well, he helped me. He was my mentor, even though I'd never met him.

Had he ever made anyone cry? Probably. He talked a lot about crybabies in *Mind Your Business*.

Wait. I made people cry. Was I a bad person?

Nothing made sense.

I made two columns on a piece of paper. One side was Good Person, and the other was Bad Person.

On the Good Person side, I wrote "Successful business professional." I crossed it out. My recent sales and investments had been terrible.

I wrote "Good brother." Then I remembered Daniel crying at dinner. I'd also yelled at him, and made him do embarrassing things, and bossed him around a lot. I crossed it out. I started to write "Good son." That wasn't true, either. Neither was "Good friend."

On the Bad Person side, I wrote "Made Dad almost cry (maybe)" and "Lied to Mom about studying and doing King Midas project." Then I added "Spied on Rachel Chambers." I crossed it out and wrote "Performed Stellar Market Research" on the Good Person side.

Could you be a good businessperson and a Good Person at the same time?

I balled up the paper in my fist.

Knock. Knock-knock. Knock-knock-knock.

It was Dad. That was our code. One. One-two. One-two-three. I loved counting even back when I was an amateur preschooler.

"One. One-two. One-two-three," I said. That meant it was okay to come in.

Dad opened the door.

"Hey, buddy," he said.

"Wait," I said. "Why are you being nice? Don't you want to strangle me?"

Dad scratched his chin like he was thinking about it. Then he smiled. "Nope," he said. "Well, maybe a light kick in the shins."

I tried not to laugh. Laughing felt wrong. I hadn't earned happiness after all the bad stuff I'd said.

"I don't think you're allowed to say that to your own kid," I said.

"Probably not," Dad agreed.

"I didn't mean it," I blurted out. "About Granddad Gronkowski not being proud of you."

Dad nodded.

I counted the silence. *One, two, three, four, five.*

"You know what, Peter?" he finally said. "Not everyone has the same definition of success."

"That's . . . huh?" I said. I'd started to say, "That's ridiculous," but that seemed like something a Bad Person would do.

"Do you know what I consider my greatest success?" Dad asked.

"Uh," I started. This was dangerous territory. "Your triple-dip chocolate chip cookies?"

"No," Dad said. "But I'm pretty proud of those, too. My biggest success is you. Daniel. Mom. My biggest success is my family."

"But . . . you don't get paid," I said.

"I don't need to get paid to feel like a success," Dad said. "My whole life, I thought my dad was a success. And he was! He loved his work and running his business. But me? I never felt like a greater success than after I got laid off."

It was official. Dad had lost his mind.

"Dad," I said slowly. "Being laid off is not a success."

Dad smiled. "I never told you, did I? Before I started at the advertising firm, I worked for your granddad. He fired me after one week."

"No way," I said.

 BUSINESS TIP: Layoffs are a business decision.

But this sounded personal. I wondered if Grand-dad Gronkowski was a Bad Person, too.

"Yup," Dad said. "He called me into his office and said, 'I think we're done here.'" He laughed again. "At first I was so mad I couldn't see straight."

I thought about the day I laid Rachel off. Was she that mad, too?

"I wanted to burn the whole place down," Dad said.

"That would have been really unprofessional," I said. "And probably an insurance nightmare."

"I practically begged him to fire me," Dad said. "I was a terrible employee. I was miserable. He did me a favor."

"A favor?" I asked.

"Yep. Your granddad sold the business to someone who really wanted it. That wasn't me." He paused. "Look, I know you don't know many stay-at-home dads. But it works for us, for our family."

I stared at him. "You're not getting another job?" I asked. "Why not?"

"Do you know how great I have it?" he said. "I love making your cupcakes. I love being here when you come home from school. Being with you guys makes me feel like a success. For your mom, working is success. For me—for us—we'd rather have less money and more time. Deciding not to work can be a business decision, too."

I asked something I'd been wanting to know for a long time.

"Dad," I said. My voice shook. "Are we poor?"

"We're okay," Dad said. "We're not rich, but we're okay. That's something you don't need to worry about."

"I do worry about it," I said. "All the time. It feels like everyone has more money than we do." *Like Ken*, I thought.

"I know, Peter," Dad said. He squeezed my shoulder. "It might seem that way. But we have more than some and less than others. That's just life."

Then I asked something even harder. I wasn't sure I wanted to know the answer.

"Do you think I'm a Bad Person?"

I picked up my crumpled list and showed it to him.

"Peter," Dad said. I held my breath. "You're more than what you do. So much more. You're a great big brother. You're creative and smart."

"I get bad grades," I said. "I might have to go to summer school."

"Smart means different things," Dad said. "People are different, period. You know how you feel comfortable talking business, but not so comfortable talking about . . . emotions?" I nodded. "Well, a lot of people are the opposite. They feel fake talking business."

"But business is in my blood," I said. "I'm not faking it."

"I know you're not," Dad said. "You don't have to."

One, two, three, four, five.

"I haven't seen Ken around lately," he said. "Did you cancel Monster Movie Night?"

"We got in a fight," I mumbled.

"Friendships, man," Dad said. "They're tough. They take work. A different kind of work."

I nodded. I'd never thought of it that way before.

"I'm sorry," I told him. "Really, really sorry." Tom Reddi says never apologize for anything. But I could make an exception for Dad.

Dad stuck out his hand. Instead, I gave him a hug. Not a corporate handshake. A real hug.

It wasn't professional. But it felt pretty good.

———•———

That night I reread the "Invest for Success" issue of *Mind Your Business.*

The Redditorial was "Monitoring Your Investments." If an investment isn't paying off, you have to make a change, move things around.

"The key," Tom wrote, "is a balanced portfolio. Make a detailed assessment of your business investments."

My life was not a balanced portfolio. I treated people like employees. My parents, my brother, Ken, Rachel. Even Mike the Unusual. I'd ruined his first comedy-slash-magic act. And I'd spoiled Clover's birthday party.

Dad was right. Friendships are like investments. They take time and energy. You have to help them grow.

Real friendships aren't business transactions. If you always treat people like employees, they'll always see you as a professional. Not as a person. Not as a friend.

28

Rachel

My whole life, I hated being invisible. Now I wished I could erase myself from the planet.

After Clover's party, I didn't go home. I couldn't. I couldn't even face Molly. Her eyes would blink up at me and make me believe everything was okay. But it wasn't.

So I ran.

I ran through the park. I ran past the Children's Museum. I ran up and down the Hill of Fun behind the library. I imagined if I ran fast enough, no one would see me. I'd be a blur, not a person who hurt people.

After a while, I almost passed out from thirst. The Reddi Mart sign flashed down the street. I checked my turtle change purse. It was so full the top didn't even close.

I had more than enough money for a bottle of water. I could probably buy the whole water section of the Reddi Mart refrigerator. But I didn't feel right spending a single penny. It was dirty money. I turned around. I deserved to suffer.

As I passed the Cash-4-Gold pawn shop, something in the window caught my eye. Something shining in a display case, with a price tag dangling from the side.

It looked exactly like Peter's watch. No . . . it *was* Peter's watch. I'd know that hunk of gold anywhere. When you clean something with a toothbrush over and over again, you develop a very close relationship.

Just like that, I went from mad at myself to mad at Peter all over again. Who cared if my money was dirty? I wanted to buy that watch. I *could* buy that watch. I could buy it and stomp all over it, just like he bought my pyrite and stomped all over my life.

I marched up the pawn shop's rickety steps. The sign on the door said CLOSED! BE BACK TOMORROW . . . MAYBE.

The sky was getting darker by the second. I had to get back soon or Dad would call the police.

The whole way home, I couldn't get that dumb

watch out of my head. I mentally smashed it into ten million tiny gold pieces.

But why was it for sale?

"Rachel!" Dad said when I walked through the front door. "Where were you? Mrs. O'Reilly said you left Clover's party hours ago. I've been worried sick."

Worried. That wouldn't last long. Soon he'd be disappointed. He'd hate me like everyone else.

"I'm sorry," I said. "Can I just hide for three minutes?"

I went to the laundry room and curled up in a basket. I didn't care that it was filled with my dirty socks and underwear. I deserved it.

After three minutes, Dad came in and knelt down beside me.

"Rachel, what happened?" he asked. "You're scaring me. Please. Talk to me."

I sat up in my basket, my face covered in snot and dirt and tears. Then I told him everything.

"I was fighting back!" I said. "I can't let someone like Peter Gronkowski win. He lies to people, he cheats people, he uses people . . . it's not fair! He can't get away with it!"

Dad held me close and rubbed my back. After a while, he said, "Rachel, this . . . lying. It doesn't sound like you."

"I don't even know who I sound like anymore," I said. I'd always wanted to just be me, to use my voice, but I was still using somebody else's. Janet March's. Gilda Stones. Peter Gronkowski's.

"I know this is a hard time," he said. "Middle school was hard for me, too. In a different way."

"Like how?" I asked.

"Just guy stuff," he said. "Getting picked on for being short."

I couldn't imagine my dad in middle school, going through guy stuff.

"Is this because . . ." Dad started. His voice trailed off.

"What?"

"Um," he said. His face was bright red. "Okay. I was about to ask if you'd gotten your period. That's the worst possible thing to ask you, right?"

Now my face felt hot. "Oh my gosh," I said. "No. I haven't gotten it yet."

"But you . . . know? About getting a period? Or is it having a period?"

I laughed. "Yes."

"Stop laughing!" he said. But he was laughing, too. "I'm doing this all wrong, aren't I?" He looked down. "I wish you had your mom."

"But I don't," I said. "I have you."

He nodded.

"Do you miss her?" I asked him.

"Oh," he said with a sigh. "Yeah." He swallowed and looked down. When he looked up, his eyes were bright and teary.

I squeezed his hand. I wanted to cry, too, so he didn't feel alone, but I didn't remember her. That's part of why I needed him. To help me remember. I wanted to know more about her so I could miss her, too.

"What would she say?" I asked. "About what I did?"

He laughed. "You know, she'd probably be proud of you in a way. You have her temper."

"She had a temper?" I said. When someone is dead, you sometimes imagine they're a perfect angel. I liked hearing about the real Mom.

"Are you kidding? She was a fighter. Once her band played at Freddy's on Main. The owner didn't pay them. She got so mad she took them to small claims court. And she won. Only one hundred dollars, but it was the principle. Hell hath no fury like a woman stiffed by a bar owner."

"She was in a *band*?"

He nodded. "Didn't I tell you that?"

I shook my head.

"I'm not used to having a temper," I said. "Revenge turned me into a menace to society."

"You know what they say, Scoots," Dad said. "Revenge is like drinking rat poison and expecting the rat to die."

I rubbed my eyes. "Huh?"

"Revenge may feel good, at first. And the other person may deserve everything you're doing and more. But when you think you're hurting them, you're only hurting yourself."

"But what are you supposed to do if people hurt you? Let them get away with it?" I asked.

"I really don't know, honey," he said.

"Aren't you supposed to know?" I asked. "You're a dad."

"I wish I had the answer," he said. "All I know is, you have to be the best you that you can be. Always. You can't sink to anyone else's level. Winners never cheat, and cheaters never win."

"Adults always say that," I said. "But adults always cheat! It's basically every single story on the news. Like that Olympic guy."

"Ah, but the chickens come home to roost," Dad said.

"What chickens?" I asked.

"It means most cheaters end up getting caught in the end. And if they don't . . . well, all you can do is make sure *you* sleep at night."

———•———

Dad didn't punish me for lying about the gold. He just said I had to read *Resolving Conflict, Face-to-Face.*

"I expect you to make things right," he said.

I didn't have to ask what that meant. I knew I had to return money to every kid I'd scammed with RC Gold. Face-to-face.

That night, Molly slept in my bed. She nuzzled me with her wet nose.

I'd ruined (almost) everything. But if I had the power to ruin things, maybe I had the power to make them better, too.

Finally, I thought. *That sounds like me.*

I fell asleep.

29
PETER

Phase One of Balancing My Life Portfolio: Do my King Midas project for school.

I had no choice. I was grounded. That was Mom's idea. She said I should never talk to Dad the way I did at dinner.

Part of being grounded was no Internet, no TV, and no businesses until I "showed dedication to my schoolwork." Mom made a good point: I'd never get into B school with my grades.

First, I had to read the King Midas story. To the end. Second, I had to present a King Midas "character study" in class.

"Piece of cake," I told Mom at breakfast. "He turns everything to gold. And my character study is easy. He's a bona fide success."

Mom snorted into her coffee. "That's not the whole story."

"What do you mean?" I asked.

"Just read it, Peter," she said.

I poured ice-cold 2 percent milk into my Peter Presents coffee mug and opened my book.

———•———

The next day, I walked into Poplar Middle School wearing donkey ears.

It was all part of the presentation. In the classroom, just like in the boardroom, or even the cul-de-sac, you have to make an entrance.

The donkey ears were giving me a headache, so I asked Ms. Hargreaves if I could go first. She nodded.

I marched to the front of the classroom.

"Greetings," I said. I waited till I had everyone's full attention. You get everyone's full attention fast when you're wearing donkey ears.

"Today I have a very special presentation." I pulled up the first slide, a drawing I made of a rich guy in a robe and crown. "This is King Midas. Everything he touched turned to gold. Sounds terrific, right?"

The next slide showed a big red X. "Wrong," I

said. "When everything you touch turns to gold, bad things happen. Bad things happened to King Midas. He couldn't eat. He couldn't drink. He even turned his own daughter to gold. That means she died. He killed his own daughter."

I paused to let that sink in for a second.

"But wait! There's more," I said. A picture of a donkey appeared. "King Midas also said he knew more about music than the god Apollo. Apollo got so mad he gave King Midas donkey ears. Then everyone saw him for the fool he really was."

A picture of a scale with two sides popped up on the screen. On one side was a photo of me in my Executive Lawn Chair, staring into the sunset. The photo crashed down onto the scale, making the other side go way up. "Before I read these stories, I thought King Midas was a bona fide success. I wanted to turn everything to gold, too. But now I see that being rich isn't everything."

Click. A picture of me, Daniel, Ken, and my parents playing cards at the beach dropped onto the other side of the scale, making both sides even. "This is a more balanced life."

I pulled up the next slide. "This is King Midas's life portfolio. It's out of balance. First, he was too greedy. He was already the king. Why would he turn everything to gold if he was already rich? Second, it's not smart to tie yourself to only one commodity. Third, he didn't invest enough time in leisure, family, and friendship. As you can see, those categories show very poor percentages. And King Midas ended up alone.

"In conclusion, too much money and gold and work can ruin your life. It doesn't solve all your problems. It just means you can buy more stuff. Stuff doesn't care about you. People do." I pointed to my ears. "And you don't want to end up like this."

The whole class clapped. Ms. Hargreaves gave me a thumbs-up.

I got an A.

Phase Two of my Life Portfolio Plan: Talk to Ken.

After my highly successful presentation, I made a pie chart to evaluate my relationships. Like King Midas, I scored poorly in the Friends and Family section.

 BUSINESS TIP: A strong person can admit weakness.

It felt weird calling Ken out of nowhere. We hadn't talked since I yelled at him for not giving me the loan.

Maybe he didn't care anymore. He had other friends. But I didn't. He knew stuff about me that nobody else did. First, my favorite monster movie. Second, how I eat pancakes only in stacks of three. Third, that I stayed in the church bathroom during Granddad's funeral. He stood outside the door so no one could come in.

"Peter?" Ken said when he answered. I forgot his EtherPhone 7 had caller ID.

"Yes," I said. I cleared my throat. "This is Peter. Peter Gronkowski."

Ken paused. "I know. You don't have to say your last name."

"Okay," I said. "Just Peter then. Hey, did I leave my remote control pickle at your house?" I knew I hadn't. I almost sold it to Harlan. I just needed something to talk about.

"Uh . . . nope," Ken said.

"Okay."

I didn't know what to say next. I was good at pretending to talk on the phone. I wasn't so good at talking on the phone for real.

I thought about Mom talking to her friends.

"So, how are things?" I asked.

"What things?" Ken replied.

"I mean, what's going on?" I said.

"Uh, I'm at my house. Eating Rice Krispy Treats."

"Oh," I said. I knew he meant real Rice Krispy Treats, not Crispy Sensation Delights. It made me feel pukey for a second. Then I remembered money isn't part of friendship. Ken didn't think I was a loser because my dad bought generic stuff. Anyway, Crispy Sensation Delights aren't that bad. "Rice Krispy Treats are good."

"Duh."

I laughed. I didn't know Ken could be nice *and* honest.

"So, uh, do you want to come over later?" I asked. I felt like I was asking my best friend out on a date.

"I don't know," Ken said. He paused. "I don't feel like doing business stuff."

"No business stuff," I said. "I'm not allowed to, anyway. We'll do something—" I swallowed. "Fun."

For a second I thought Ken dropped the phone. "Really?" he asked.

"Yeah," I said. "I'll invite Mike, too. We can play

a game or watch a monster movie or something."
Maybe it was time to open up the Inner Circle. I
owed Mike an apology, too, for ruining his comedy-
slash-magic show.

"Cool," Ken said. "But no Monopoly."

Dear Clover,

It's ~~not~~ okay if you hate me. I ~~don't~~ deserve it. I'm sorry. Please forgive me.

Hey Clover,

Remember when I dared you to jump out of your bedroom window and your nightgown ripped and you screamed and your dad called the police and the fire department came and you hid in the bushes? That was funny. Will you forgive me now?

Hi,

Okay, if you're not going to answer my calls, I might as well tell the truth. I'm sorry I lied. But I'm tired of pretending everything is okay. I'm tired of you stealing my jokes. I'm tired of you talking for me and over me, even if I kind of do let it happen, so maybe it's my fault, too. I'm tired of writing all your acceptance speeches, especially if it's a contest that I lost! It's like losing all over again. What's the opposite of a consolation prize? That's what it feels like. A discouragement punishment (I used a thesaurus for that).

Clover,

Sometimes it's hard to be your best friend.

30

Rachel

People used to ignore me, but not because I did anything wrong. Now it was on purpose. I couldn't even return anyone's money because no one would talk to me. Not even Clover.

I'd been calling her for days. Mrs. O'Reilly always said she was washing her hair. Clover has a lot of hair, but I didn't believe it . . . mostly because I heard her saying, "I don't talk to traitors!" in the background.

Now I ate lunch in the janitor's closet. I felt like Cyrano in the pigpen, only I deserved it.

I pulled up a step stool between two mops and started writing. It had been a while, but now I had nothing but time (and mops).

CYRANO'S REVENGE

CHAPTER LXX

Queen Cyrano grabbed her sister Tulip's skirt, sobbing into its fraying hem.

"I beg your forgiveness, dear sister!" Cyrano pleaded.

"Dear sister!" Tulip scoffed. "You kept me—us—from the family fortune! I lived in a rundown shack with my family. My husband, Sir Michael the Strange, died penniless! And now I am a poor widow, caring for quadruplets. Alone."

Being hurt sometimes makes you hurt other people. First Pouncey betrayed Cyrano, then Cyrano betrayed Tulip. But Tulip hurt Cyrano when she got married and left her behind. And maybe somebody hurt Pouncey before he betrayed Cyrano. Where does the hurt start, and where does it end?

I chewed my pen. In a weird way, maybe I was hurting Cyrano because I hurt, too.

No one is perfect. Not Tulip, not Clover, not Cyrano, not me. Especially not me.

I owed Clover an apology, but sorry wasn't enough. I owed her the truth.

———•———

On Saturday, I went to Clover's house bright and early (but not too early, because she's not a morning person).

Mrs. O'Reilly answered the door.

"Hi, Rachel," she said. She carried baby Juniper on her hip while Daisy grabbed at her ankles.

"Is Clover here?" I asked. "Or is she still washing her hair?"

Mrs. O'Reilly smiled. "*Clover!*" she yelled. Maybe excessive earwax is genetic.

"What?" Clover said, running to the door. Her hair was dry. She stopped when she saw me.

"I'll leave you girls alone," Mrs. O'Reilly said, wandering off.

"What do you want?" Clover said. She folded her arms across her chest.

"I want to say I'm sorry," I said. It wasn't as dramatic as I'd imagined. I didn't sob into her skirt. She wasn't wearing a skirt, anyway. Just cat pajamas.

"You should be sorry," Clover said. "I stood up for you. You embarrassed me. You made me look like a liar."

"I know," I said. "I just . . . I don't want you to be mad at me."

"And you ruined my birthday party! You only turn twelve once!"

"I know," I said again. "Look, can I say something?"

She didn't flinch.

"Okay," I said. "So there's you and me. When it's just us two, we're in this happy, unpoppable bubble."

Clover wrinkled her nose. "A bubble?"

"Right. A bubble. But when it's us with other people, the bubble pops, and I . . . disappear. It's like I need the bubble to survive. But you don't need the bubble at all. I mean, you think the bubble is fine, but you also love the world outside the bubble. Because you're popular and everyone listens to you. But I feel like no one listens to me."

"I do!" Clover said. "I listen to you!"

"Sometimes you don't," I said softly.

Clover's jaw dropped. She looked sad and angry at the same time.

"I'm sorry," I said. "I don't want to hurt you more. But I have to tell you the whole truth, because you're my best friend. At least I hope you are."

I took a deep breath.

"That's why I turned into a pyrite monster," I said. "Because I had to pop the bubble myself. But I guess I popped it too hard, because I hurt you. And I never meant to do that."

Clover paused. "You really *did* turn into a pyrite monster."

"I know!" I said, throwing up my hands. "I just said that! So what do you want to do? Punch me? Throw a pie in my face? I don't care. I just want you to forgive me."

Clover's lip twitched like she was trying not to laugh. She uncrossed her arms. "Okay. Yes. I want to throw a pie in your face."

"Ha. Ha," I said.

"No joke," Clover said. "Let me throw a pie in your face, and I'll forgive you."

"Are you serious?"

"Totally," she said. "And by the way, you're

wrong." She looked down. "I *do* need our bubble."

My throat closed up. I swallowed hard and smiled.

At my house, I found an old pie crust in the back of the pantry and an ancient can of whipped cream in the refrigerator. I sprayed cream into the crust until the can was empty.

I went back to Clover's.

"Here," I said, handing her the pie.

"We'll do it on my front lawn, so everyone can see," Clover said, her eyes sparkling. She stuck her finger in the pie and tasted it. "Revenge is sweet!"

I didn't tell her what Dad said about revenge being like poisoning yourself. Clover was right. Sometimes, revenge was sweet. I also didn't tell her that the whipped cream expired three days ago.

"Fine," I said. "Hit me with your best pie."

Clover snorted. She wound up like a not-so-skilled softball pitcher (she's an artist, not an athlete), then *slam!*

"Eeeeeee!" I shrieked. Cream dripped down my face. "It's cold! And slimy!"

"I can't believe . . . you let me . . . *do that!*" Clover clutched her stomach and rolled to the ground, howling. "Your eyes look like holes!"

"All right, all right," I said. Now I couldn't stop laughing, thinking about my hole-eyes.

I wiped my face with a towel. When I looked up, I saw every kid in the cul-de-sac on their front porches, staring at me. Every kid except Peter Gronkowski.

The old me would have wanted to hide in an underground shelter for eternity. But the new me shrugged. That's just part of living in a cul-de-sac. Everybody can see your business, and sometimes that's a good thing. It keeps you honest.

I walked home later, my clothes and hair covered in whipped cream.

Dad met me at the door. He opened his mouth, then closed it, then opened it again.

"Clover and I made up," I said.

———•———

I took a long shower to wash off every bit of whipped cream. I put on my pajamas and reached for my pyrite ring on the dresser.

It wasn't there.

I searched under clean and dirty clothes.

It was gone. I couldn't breathe.

I ran into the bathroom. A flash in the mirror caught my eye.

My ring. It was on the bathroom sink, as sparkly as ever. I picked it up and held it against my heart.

I thought about Peter's watch. Why did I even care? He sold it to a pawn shop. That's how much *he* cared.

But that watch was practically the only thing he loved.

Then I understood. He didn't want the money. He needed it. That's how he could afford the pyrite at the Children's Museum.

He was desperate.

I'd been desperate, too. I mean, I spray-painted rocks. Desperation makes you do bizarre things.

In a weird way, I admired him. I could never, ever sell my mom's ring. I'd only worn it for a few weeks, but now it was a part of me, of her, of us. It was our connection.

Selling that watch might have been the hardest thing Peter Gronkowski had ever done. And after all of that, he was probably broke.

I twirled my ring, and a brilliant idea jumped into my brain.

The next morning, I told Dad my plan.

"You want to make how many cream pies?" he asked.

"Twenty," I said. "No, thirty."

"I can help, but I'm better with pasta than pastries," he said. "Are you opening a bakery?"

"No," I said. "Every kid in the cul-de-sac hates me right now, except for Clover. If I let them get revenge, maybe they won't hate me anymore. So they can get their money back, or they can throw a pie in my face. I'll donate whatever money is left over to charity."

"And what charity is that?" Dad asked.

I laughed. Usually *he* confuses *me*. "I want to help someone in our cul-de-sac," I said. "Someone who needs it more than I do."

Clover offered to be the official sign maker and wagon puller for Pie-Right Industries.

"And you don't even have to pay me!" she said. "I'm sick of money, anyway."

So was I.

We loaded up the Pie-Right wagon with thirty cream pies.

Our first stop was Mike the Unusual's house. He answered the door with his headphones on.

"I'm sorry for lying to you, Mike," I said. "I owe you . . ." I checked my notebook. "Fifteen dollars."

"Cool," Mike said.

"Isn't she sooooo cool?" Clover said, batting her eyes. I elbowed her in the ribs.

"You get a choice," I said. "The customer should always have a choice. I'll give you your money back, or you can get revenge on me. You can throw a pie in my face. Right now. And I'll donate your money to a good cause."

Mike scratched his chin. "What's the good cause?"

"Helping someone in our community," I said. "The person will remain anonymous."

"I don't know," Mike said. "Why should I trust you?"

I gulped. He was right. Trust was way harder to earn back than money. That was the price of betrayal.

"It's up to you," I said. "But all I can tell you is that I promise. I really do. This is your chance to get revenge for all the right reasons."

Clover pointed to the Pie-Right sign.

Mike shrugged. "Can I pick out the pie?"

I smiled. "Any one you want."

As we left Mike's house, I asked Clover, "Should I change my clothes between stops?" I was covered head to toe in whipped cream.

Clover narrowed her eyes. "You look more pathetic this way. I like it."

We rang Mel Chang's doorbell.

Before I could even open my mouth, Mel said, "I'll do the pie."

"How did you—" I started.

"It's my job," Mel said. "I know everything."

Mel wound up before her pitch. She had a surprisingly strong pie-throwing arm.

"Have you done this before?" I sputtered through a mouthful of whipped cream. She grinned.

After our pie session, Mel snapped a few pictures for her blog. "Perf," she said. "Well done, Rach."

For the first time in a while, I felt proud of myself.

Clover and I wheeled the Pie-Right wagon around till dusk. It took a long time because we had to go all the way to Fountain's Spout. It's pretty amazing that kids came from that far away for RC Gold. Someday, I hoped that many people would want to read my books. Hopefully they wouldn't want to throw pies in my face.

A few kids wanted their money back. But most of them chose the pie. A handful even paid me more money to throw an extra one.

My stomach grumbled as we turned into our cul-de-sac. It was almost dinnertime. We passed Peter's house on the way to mine.

"Creepy," Clover whispered, pointing up.

Peter was sitting by his bedroom window with a magazine over his face. He poked his head over the top to peek at us. Then he covered his face again.

"I'd probably stare if I saw some girl covered head to toe in whipped cream, too," I said.

He didn't look creepy to me. He looked sad. And lonely. As much as he'd hurt me, I guess I'd hurt him, too.

"Time for me to do a good thing," I told Clover. "Oh, and take a shower."

31
PETER

Phase Three of my Life Portfolio Plan: Tell Dad the truth about my watch. If I wanted to be a better businessman, and a better man period, I needed to come clean.

I downed an extra Success Snack to psych myself up. I fluttered my eyelids. Then I went to see Dad in the garden.

"You know how I told Mom that Granddad's watch was being cleaned?" I asked him.

"Yup," Dad said, picking at some roots in the turnip patch.

"I lied," I said.

Dad stopped shoveling. He looked up from the turnips.

"I sold it to Harlan's Cash-4-Gold Pawn Shop," I

continued. "I used the money to buy all the pyrite from the Children's Museum so I could beat Rachel."

It's one thing to hear about Tom Reddi doing a hostile takeover. But when you do it yourself, and you tell someone what you did, it seems pretty terrible. I swallowed. Hard.

"Peter," Dad said in a low, quiet voice. "Okay. We'll get it back."

"I'll make it up to you, Dad," I said. "I'm sorry."

I'd really screwed up. All along, I was trying to help our family. But I got off track. I made things worse. And now we had to buy a watch we already owned, with money we didn't have.

———◦———

Dad didn't say much on the way to the pawn shop. Neither did I.

We walked up Harlan's creaky wooden steps. The bells jangled as I pushed the door open. The hair on my arms stood up.

Harlan was labeling boxes behind the register. "Greetings, my good men," he said. "What can I do ya for?"

"Peter?" Dad said. He nudged me forward.

"Yeah," I said. I cleared my throat. "Um, we want

to buy the gold watch I sold you. My watch. My . . . granddad's watch."

"I remember," Harlan said. He wiped his hands on a towel and came around the counter. "Bad news, kid. I sold that watch yesterday."

A real professional would have told Dad about the watch sooner. A real professional would have never gotten into this situation.

"I'm sorry, sport," Harlan said. "I wish I could help you out."

Harlan shoved his hands in the pockets of his dirty black jeans. His eyes looked sad. He didn't look very professional, but I knew he meant what he said.

"Rick," Harlan said to Dad. "If I'd known it was your dad's, I never would have—"

I held up my hand. "It was me," I said. "My fault." I felt like I was speaking a different language. Dad put a hand on my shoulder.

"Thanks, Harlan," Dad said. He led me outside.

I squinted in the sunshine. A lump grew in my throat. It didn't feel like a glitter allergy. I swallowed a lot to make it go away. But the lump got bigger.

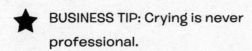 **BUSINESS TIP: Crying is never professional.**

I wasn't a professional. I was a kid. An ordinary, amateur kid.

I cried. I cried, in public, outside the Cash-4-Gold Pawn Shop, outside the Reddi Mart, where anyone could see me, including Tom Reddi himself.

Dad hugged me. "I'm proud of you, Peter," he said. "Everything will be okay. It's just a watch."

It wasn't. Not to me. At first I only wanted it because it was gold. Now I wanted it because it was my granddad's. And he was gone.

Now the watch was gone, too.

CYRANO'S REVENGE

CHAPTER XC

The bell chimed four. It was time for Pouncey the craven copycat's execution.

Queen Cyrano sat upon her throne, her loyal pigs beside her.

The guards brought Pouncey before Queen Cyrano in chains. His eyes had the sad, bewildered look of a man about to lose his head.

At first sight she felt the familiar rush of fury. But to Queen Cyrano's surprise, her rage burned out as quickly as it came. That kind of anger could not last. It could only destroy the person who felt it.

Queen Cyrano had always secretly blamed Pouncey for her parents' deaths. Now she understood that only Fate was responsible. It wasn't Pouncey's fault. It wasn't anyone's fault.

But his death would surely be hers.

Well, not entirely. He was the one who stole her poetry and treated her like a common pig (although to Cyrano, no pigs were common). But Queen Cyrano had a choice. She could choose forgiveness.

Queen Cyrano thought of Tulip, her dear sister. Tulip had forgiven her. Did not everyone deserve the same chance?

Pouncey kneeled before her.

Queen Cyrano extended her hand. "Rise," she said.

32

Rachel

I stood by Peter's mailbox for a long time. I wanted to shove the envelope in and never say another word about it.

That would have been a whole lot easier.

But something inside me said to do what I had to do in person, because that was the hard thing. And easy didn't feel like me, anyway. Sometimes, being afraid means you need to go toward the scary thing rather than running away from it.

I wasn't even mad at Peter anymore. Not really. Maybe 33 percent mad. But the other 67 percent . . . that part knew why he did what he did. Winning feels good, until you're winning for the wrong reasons.

I rang Peter's doorbell. I held the envelope in both hands to keep them from shaking.

Daniel answered.

"Puppet!" Daniel said. "Can I throw a pie in your face?"

"It's Rachel," I said. "And not today. Is Peter here?"

"*Peter!!!!!!*"

I heard footsteps.

"Daniel," Peter said as he came down the stairs. "Shouting is unprof—"

He stopped mid-step and cleared his throat.

"How can I help you?" he asked.

"I have something for you," I said. I showed him the envelope.

Daniel tried to snatch it from me. "I'm the package taker," he said.

"I'll handle this, Daniel," Peter said. "You're excused."

"Woohoo!" Daniel raced down the hall in monkey-socked feet.

Peter came all the way downstairs. I gave him the envelope, and he held it up to the light.

"What is this?" he asked. "It's heavy." He raised an eyebrow. "It's not lemonade. Or a carrot."

"No," I said. "I promise."

Peter took a letter opener from the hall table and cut through the top of the envelope.

Sunshine poured into the hallway through sparkling clean windows. It made the gold watch look even brighter. (Okay, so I cleaned it one last time. Old habits die hard.)

Peter turned pale. For a second I worried the heart attack rumors were true.

"This is my watch," he said.

"Yeah."

"Wait. You're the one? You bought it from the pawn shop?" Peter asked. I could practically see his brain circuits exploding. "How much do you want?"

"Nothing," I said. "Well, not nothing. I want you to start paying your interns. And stop stealing people's ideas. And stop spying. And stop sabotaging other people's businesses. But I don't want money."

He paused. "Why are you being nice to me?"

It was a fair question.

"Because," I said. "I'm tired of being mean. Business doesn't have to make you mean. Business can be good. People can be good, too. Look, we both got our hands dirty. We can wash them. We can start over," I said. "Did I just make that up? Whoa. Maybe it came from my dad. I don't know. He's a librarian. I guess you know that already."

I'd never said that many words out loud at once in my whole life, especially to Peter Gronkowski. He looked dizzy.

"Anyway," I said. "It's a gift."

"A gift," Peter repeated.

"Right," I said. "It's not business. It's personal."

I grinned and walked away. It was kind of fun leaving Peter Gronkowski speechless.

33
PETER

7:59 a.m. My Corner Office.

Knock. Knock. Knock.

"Daniel," I said. "One minute early. I'm impressed. Have a seat." I pointed to my Executive Lawn Chair.

He sat down slowly, like I'd put a whoopee cushion on it.

"Refreshments?" I said. I handed him an ice cream sandwich.

He grinned and took a giant bite. He looked so happy it almost made me sad. I'd been a real jerk. Daniel always believed in me, even if I didn't deserve it. Lucky for me, four-year-olds don't hold grudges.

"Let's get down to brass tacks," I said. "I need to pick your brain."

Daniel's eyes bugged out. "No, Peter," he whispered. "Ew."

"That means I need to ask you something," I said. "I need you to be my consultant."

I cleared my throat. I'd never felt awkward in a business presentation before. Especially not in front of a four-year-old.

"Daniel," I said. "How do you . . . talk to girls?"

"Huh?" he asked.

"You're a married man," I said. "You have field experience. With Daisy. I want to apologize to Rachel Chambers. How would you advise me to move forward?"

Daniel chewed his ice cream sandwich slowly.

"What do you say to Daisy when you do something wrong?" I asked.

"I say, 'I'm sorry.'"

"That's it?"

"And 'I like your braids.'"

"Rachel doesn't have braids."

"And 'I love you.'"

"I don't love her," I said.

He shrugged. "You can give her a valentine. A friend valentine."

I was starting to regret asking Daniel for advice. But suddenly, out of nowhere, my head started to sweat. He wasn't such an amateur after all.

"Daniel, you just helped me think outside the box," I said. "I'd like you to promote you to the Inner Circle."

I stuck out my hand. He shook it. Melted ice cream dripped all over my wrist. I didn't even make him clean it up.

"Yay!" Daniel said. "Now will you tell me how you hatched from a golden egg?"

PERFORMANCE REVIEW

Dear Rachel,

A good boss gives Performance Reviews to employees. I was not a good boss. I apologize for the delay.

As I'm sure you're aware, the most innovative bosses in the world review themselves as well as their employees. I'll start with me:

ME:

Before you were my intern, I thought I had only strengths: extreme professionalism, sales experience, street-smart sophistication, etc. But I learned I had weaknesses, too. One was that I only talked about other people's weaknesses. I had it backward. People aren't motivated by feeling bad about themselves. A good boss builds people up. When you motivate people with positive things, they work harder. That's called positive psychology. I read all about it in this book I got from your dad. It's called *Good Job!* He gave me a terrific deal on an extended library loan.

BUSINESS TIP (*from me, not Tom Reddi*): Weaknesses can be strengths.

You can't grow without knowing what to work on. Overall, I'd classify myself as On Probation and Needs Much Improvement.

YOU:

As mentioned above, I've never told anyone their strengths before. Please be patient as I embark on this new adventure.

You increased sales 35 percent, elevated my business model, and showcased management-level decision-making abilities. You even wrote fortunes. You're a tremendous businesswoman with innovative insight into what consumers want: an engaging experience.

Your biggest strength is being thoughtful. Sometimes it's a good business decision not to talk all the time. It makes what you say more important.

As for your weaknesses, you can handle that yourself. First, I'm practicing positive psychology. Second, I'm not your boss anymore. Third, I don't want to make you mad. That was not a good business decision.

Bottom line: You taught me more than I taught you.

 BUSINESS TIP: That is the sign of a great employee. And a great person.

In the future, I'd be honored to write you a letter of recommendation.

Regards,

Peter

CYRANO'S REVENGE

CHAPTER XCIX:
THE FINAL CHAPTER

Queen Cyrano was Queen no more. She apologized to the people of Foggy Glen for her greed and returned the unlawful "moo taxes" she had charged them for keeping loud cows. Then she donated her crown, her gowns woven from the fruits of the most talented silkworms, even her prized Elephant Emerald, to her former subjects. In exchange, they let her keep her head—and her pigs.

"Most things we value, they are just things," Cyrano told them. "I am—we are—more than this. Our worth is greater than any gold at rainbow's end."

Cyrano did keep one worldly token until the moment she drew her very last breath at the age of 106. A sculpture of a barn dog, made from the remains of a tattered, straw-stuffed pillow. Tulip, her dear sister, had made it for Cyrano just before she was trampled in the tragic Foggy Glen Cow Stampede. The dog reminded Cyrano of simpler times at her parents' barn, when only love mattered. It was all Cyrano had left in the end, and it was all she needed.

"Forgiveness is the greatest gift," Cyrano whispered as her world grew dark.

AUDITION NOTICE!

NEXT FRIDAY AT 4:00 P.M.!

From the author of acclaimed novel *Cyrano's Revenge* comes . . . *Cyrano's Revenge: The Play*.

Cyrano's Revenge is the tale of Cyrano, a young, misunderstood girl of secret royal descent. Watch as she learns that revenge (and royalty) is not all it's cracked up to be.

Stage fright? Never fear. *Cyrano's Revenge* is a traveling production performed only on driveways.

Director Rachel Chambers seeks local talent of all ages, abilities, and confidence levels.

34

Rachel

"I still can't believe you kill me off," Clover said. "That's so mean."

"It's a compliment," I said for the hundred thousandth time. "Tulip is a hero. A symbol."

"A dead symbol," she said. "Cyrano gets to live to be one hundred and six!" She crossed her arms and yawned.

I didn't totally blame her for being cranky. It was early. Because we rehearse in my driveway, we start around 6:30 a.m. and stop when it gets too hot. Clover and I made a deal: she would be in my play, but only if she could rehearse in her pajamas.

I sat up tall in the #1 DIRECTOR chair Clover made me for my birthday.

"Let's get back to my notes," I said. "Gabby, I need

you to work on your lines. You said, 'Forgiveness is a present' again."

"It is," Gabby said. She was wearing tree frog pajamas, just like the ones Clover wore yesterday.

"The line is 'Forgiveness is a gift,'" I said.

"Same thing," Gabby said. Her eyebrows formed a perfectly straight line, like they were daring me to disagree with her. Gabby has extremely expressive eyebrows. They're a big reason I cast her as the star.

"Not really," I said. Being both a writer and a director is not easy, especially when you and your cast have "creative differences."

After I finished *Cyrano's Revenge: The Book*, I turned it into a play. I have a lot of free time now that it's summer and I'm not trying to get revenge. I also found out you can win Pulitzer Prizes for books *and* plays.

The best part about writing is that I don't keep it a secret anymore. (Most of it. I still write secret things, just for me.) And writing a play means you get to use your voice and other people can use their voices to make yours come to life. It's pretty cool.

But sometimes, I wish they wouldn't use their voices *quite* so much.

"How are costumes coming, Susie?" I asked. In my short time as a director, I've learned that changing the subject helps keep people focused and on track.

"Oooh! I have lots of designive patterns," she said. Her pajamas matched Gabby's. "First, Cyrano wears cow pajamas. Then when she's queen, she'll change into crown ones. They're an amazing color of purple."

Susie decided that everyone's real costumes should be pajamas, too. Another director-lesson I've learned is to pick your battles.

"What about me?" Clover asked.

Susie checked her notes. "Glitter cats," she said.

Clover grinned.

"Until you die," Susie went on. "Then skulls."

Clover frowned.

"Excellent," I said. "And Ken?"

"Yeah?" he asked, his ears burning red.

"Great job on Pouncey's monologue," I said. "Your projection has really improved."

He grinned.

"That's all, folks." I closed my director's notebook.

Next door, Peter stepped out of his house carrying his Executive Lawn Chair.

He looks different now. I can't figure out why. He wears the same clothes. His hair is still parted. His steps are even more gigantic than they used to be. But he's not a great white shark. I mean, he's definitely a blue whale or some other huge ocean creature. But he doesn't seem so hungry for blood. Maybe he's a mammal after all.

Peter unfolded his chair and looked over.

I waved at him. He waved back.

35
PETER

8:29 a.m. Back in business.

Summer. My busy season. I was in my Executive Lawn Chair and in my element: running a successful business operation.

But this wasn't my typical venture. I was working pro bono. That means for free. Mom does it sometimes as a lawyer.

Lots of business professionals are millionaires and billionaires. But the really successful ones help other people. They're called philanthropists. Guys like Warren Buffett, Bill Gates . . . the list goes on.

I decided to be a philanthropist in my cul-de-sac. My cul-de-sac is my community. For any of us to succeed, we need to help each other out. I'm a leader. That's what leaders do. They gather the team and bring them back together.

I didn't come up with that. First, I don't say the word "chic." Second, that was the headline of Mel Chang's First Day of Summer blog entry.

My new business helps kids come up with top-notch business proposals. Clover O'Reilly sells re-purposed pyrite art. Her motto is: "Pyrite is dead. Transform your pyrite into something cool and ALIVE with local artist Clover O'Reilly." I'm her angel investor. I gave her all the pyrite I didn't sell. And Mel Chang is in serious talks to launch a ponytail holder startup.

I even help younger entrepreneurs. I'm proud to say I helped Gabby Jonas balance her Life Portfolio. She now has time for karate, camping, acting, *and* reading the entire Balloon Animal Mystery series. Daniel's working on a passion project. He offers free lawn break-dancing classes to new business owners to help with stress management.

Oh. I've also expanded my business services to place locally made goods in locally owned stores. My first client was Dad. He's been selling Gronkowski's Goodies cookies and cupcakes exclusively in the Cone Zone.

I brokered the deal myself, but not with Tom Reddi. He doesn't own the Cone Zone anymore. He's in jail. Turns out he did a lot of unprofessional things. He was the guy Mom prosecuted in her trial. She didn't tell me at first. She didn't want to upset me.

Seeing my mentor on TV in an orange jumpsuit and handcuffs was surprising. Not in a good way. But then I realized I didn't even know him. I thought I did because I read his magazine, but I didn't. Not really. I only knew what he wanted me and other people to see.

I still read *Mind Your Business*. It's not the same, though. First, it was bought out by a company called Janet March Publications. Second, there are no Redditorials.

Other stuff has changed, too. Rachel Chambers is some kind of director. She also writes a Business Ethics column for Mel Chang's blog. It's pretty good. Sometimes it's better than *Mind Your Business*.

I checked the official Peter Presents timepiece. 9:12 a.m.

Scott MacGregor strolled over from across the street.

"You're late," I told him. "Business tip: Be on time for meetings. Especially pro bono meetings.

One more tip, pro bono: Don't wear board shorts to a board meeting."

Scott nodded. "Sorry, Peter."

I folded my fingers into a Power Tent. "What's your business proposal?"

He pulled a lime green folder out of his backpack. It matched his shorts. "I want to propose a beverage business."

I swallowed a groan. My business is called "Think Outside the Lemonade Stand," but most proposals I hear are still about lemonade. As Mr. Chambers says, "Rome wasn't built in a day."

Scott opened his folder and looked me dead straight in the eye. "What about limeade?" he asked.

I raised an eyebrow. "I'm listening."

Acknowledgments

Thanks to all my families (Jones, LeReche, Mincks, and Ross) for their support, with extra thanks to my endlessly inspiring nieces and nephews. Thanks to my kind, wise agent, Steve Malk, and the outstanding Hannah Mann for their patience and guidance. Thanks to Laura Park and all the talented folks at Viking for bringing Poplar Lane to life. I owe so much to my warm and brilliant editor, Joanna Cárdenas, who pushed me to honor truth in comedy and ensured that every character felt real.

I finished the first draft of this book two days before I had my daughter and presented it to my husband with a comically large red bow (the book, not the baby). Amid sleepless nights and napless days, he found time to read it. Thank you, Scott, for your patience, flexibility, and punchline assistance. Mattie, thank you for letting me smell your head when I didn't think I could write another word. Reesie, thank you for being the best therapy dog on the planet.

And finally, thanks to the boy on Dayton Street who sold me a rock.

It's election season at
Poplar Middle School and
the competition is *fierce*!
Who will rule the school?

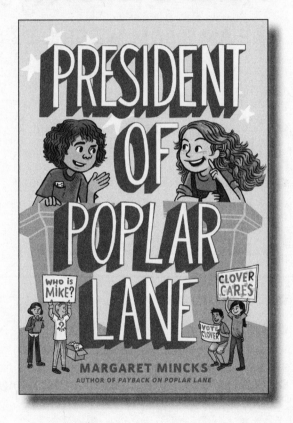

Clover O'Reilly's

DREAM ROOM WISH LIST

Paint (by wall):

- ❀ Walls one, two, and three: Eggplant Tangerine Dream

- ❀ Wall four (the Mood Wall): chalkboard paint

Furniture and Accessories:

- ❀ Beaded curtains

- ❀ No bed (soooo boring)—piles of mismatched pillows

- ❀ Sewing machine for curtains and pillows (do these still exist?)

- ❀ Easel and splat mat

Dream Room Layout:

- 🌸 Sketching corner
- 🌸 Painting corner
- 🌸 Sculpture corner
- 🌸 Mixed-media corner

Miscellaneous Essential Items:

- 🌸 sewing machine (??)
- 🌸 Three jars of gold glitter (at least)
- 🌸 Three bottles of gold glitter glue
- 🌸 Two smocks with pockets
- 🌸 Palette for mixing paints
- 🌸 Paintbrushes
- 🌸 Molding clay
- 🌸 Posters and markers for DO NOT DISTURB—ARTIST AT WORK sign (NO SISTERS ALLOWED on flip side?)

1

Clover

I took one last, deep breath. Don't worry, I wasn't about to die. It was just my last breath of roommate-oxygen. The last time I'd ever be surrounded by the smell of my older sister Violet's Vanilla Angel Rain-shower body spray.

Soon the air would be filled with another odor. (Not body odor. Ew!) The glorious odor of paint: Eggplant Tangerine Dream. It's a custom color, which means I invented it. Sometimes you can't find what you're looking for, so you have to make up something new.

If I had to wait twelve years and 150 days to get my own room, I wasn't picking some boring color off the shelf at Homer's Goods Emporium.

"Clover!" Mom yelled up the stairs.

I grabbed my Dream Room Inspiration Folder—stuffed with pictures, sketches, paint swatches, and my wish list—and raced outside.

Today would be a super great day. First, we were going to the Pancake Jamboree. If there was anything I loved as much as having my own room, it was breakfast food. Then we were going to Homer's for the paint.

Then it was only two more days till I started seventh grade. It was like a new me was blossoming from a cocoon, if cocoons had blossoms.

I love school for way too many reasons to mention, but mostly because all my friends are there. And Mike the Unusual, the cutest boy alive. Plus I'm in the Random Acts of Artness Club this year. Plus *plus*, new school supplies—crayons, sharpened pencils, notebook paper—are just so *visceral*. I learned that word from my best friend, Rachel. She reads a lot. "Visceral" means that something connects with your feelings. It's the perfect word for me because I have a *lot* of feelings.

I slid open the side door of the van and inhaled Vanilla Angel Rainshower. Violet was rubbing lotion up and down her arms. I gagged.

Sometimes having a mega-strong sense of smell can be a curse, not just a blessing. I must have a sensitive nose because I have a lot of earwax. I've read that when one sense is weak your other senses have to be extra strong to make up for it. In that way I'm kind of like Beethoven, even though I don't play the piano.

"I don't want to wear a shirt!" my little sister Daisy wailed. Baby Juniper wailed, too, because she copies everything Daisy does.

"You have to wear a shirt to the Pancake Jamboree," Dad said as he started the car.

Daisy and Juniper sat strapped into their car seats in the first row, with Juniper still facing backward. The second row was Dahlia and me.

"Pancakes are very . . . typical," Violet announced, filing her nails. To Violet, anything "very typical" is bad.

Violet got to sit by herself in the optional third row. When you're in a family with five kids, you don't get many options. But if anyone does, it's Violet. Not only does she get her own row, she's also getting her own room like me *and* she gets to wear makeup. She's not as artistic as I am, but today she had on three different colors of cat-eye eyeliner. I'm mature enough to admit it looked cool.

Honestly, I'm scared to try three eyeliner colors, because that's six chances to poke my eye out (since I have two eyes). Violet's beauty routines are dangerous. We both have curly red hair, but Violet wakes up super early to make hers straight. The last time I used her flat iron, I almost burned my hair off.

So, back to pancakes. The Pancake Jamboree is at Town Hall. We live close enough to walk, but we had to drive because we were hauling a ton of Mom's campaign signs. She was running for Poplar School Board against a man named Rocket Shipley. His real name is William, but Mom says he made up a nickname for himself so he can be "more memorable." I didn't know you could make up nicknames for yourself when you were an adult.

Clover is already a memorable name. But if I wanted to be even *more* memorable, I would be Clover "Anastasia Emerald" O'Reilly.

"Mom, are you gonna win the selection?" Dahlia asked.

"It's called a special election," I said.

"Why is it special?" she asked.

"Because a guy who was on the school board went to jail, and they have to fill his spot," I said.

Dahlia gasped. "Why did he go to jail?"

"Because he stole a bunch of money and lied," said Violet.

"If you steal and lie, then you go to jail?" Dahlia asked.

"Yup," Violet said.

Daisy burst into tears. "I don't want to go to jail," she said.

"Why would you go to jail?" Mom asked.

"I stole Violet's makeup!" she wailed. She pulled a pan of Vice City eye shadow out of her Pet-a-Pony purse.

"Oh boy," said Violet. "You'd better give it back."

"I'm not a boy!" Daisy cried even harder.

"No one's going to jail," Dad said.

"Some people go to jail," Dahlia said. "Or else jail would be empty."

"No one in *this car* is going to jail," Dad said.

"Yet," muttered Violet.

"There are different kinds of lies," Mom said. "There are little lies that don't really matter. And then there are big-deal lies."

"What's a little lie and what's a big-deal lie?" Daisy asked.

"A little lie is like when Mom told the people at Fun World you were still two so you could get in for free. Or is that a big deal?" Dahlia asked.

"It's . . . complicated," Mom said.

"I'll still vote for you, Mom," Dahlia said. "Even though you lied."

"Me too, Mommy," Daisy said.

"I'm voting for her first," Dahlia said. "In my heart."

Daisy's face turned red. She was on the verge of her second breakdown of the car ride until Mom reached back and squeezed her foot.

I rifled through my Dream Room Inspiration Folder. Dahlia snatched it right out of my hand.

"Hey!" I yelled. Magazine clippings and paint swatches scattered all over the floor, which was mostly covered in half-munched crackers and decaying French fries.

"Hay is for horses!" Dahlia said.

"Neigh!" said Daisy.

"No, *hay*!" Dahlia said.

"*No, hay neigh!*" said Juniper, clapping.

"Clover, can you take it down a notch?" Mom asked.

"Why is this my fault?" I asked. "I'm the victim!"

"Please," said Violet. I turned around to stick my tongue out at her. Like she could hear anything with her giant pink-skull headphones (which I also admit were truly awesome).

Mom rubbed her temples. Dad massaged her shoulder with his non-driving arm as he pulled into the parking lot.

Violet kicked the back of my seat. I turned around to glare at her, but the worry on her face stopped me. She nodded toward the front.

I turned back around. My parents were giggling.

Giggling is a signal. It *means something*.

"I'm starving," Mom said, rubbing her belly. Dad touched the hand on Mom's belly.

Giggles. Starvation. Belly pats.

Oh no. Not again.

Violet's eyes flashed with the same fear that bubbled in my chest.

We knew what was coming. We'd been here before. We were veterans in the Older Sister Alliance, even though Violet doesn't talk about that anymore. I guess you don't need sisters when you get to high school.

"Girls, we have wonderful news," Dad said.

I sunk down in my seat.

Violet groaned.

"We're having a baby!" Mom said.

"A *baby*?!" yelled Dahlia.

"A *what*?!" screamed Daisy. Clogged ears must be hereditary.

Juniper tried to scream "A *what*?!" like Daisy, but instead she scared herself and started crying.

"This cannot be true," I said. "You said the shop was closed for business!"

Our life was chaos already. Weren't there enough kids in this van? Did they really need more?

"It was a bit of a surprise," Mom said. "And did I really call myself a shop?"

"I need details!" I said.

"I don't," Violet muttered.

"There wasn't really a plan," Dad explained. He pulled into the Town Hall parking lot. "Aren't you guys excited?"

Wonderful. Excited. Parent code words telling me how I was supposed to feel.

"A *baby*!" Daisy screamed again.

Daisy didn't get it. She thought a baby meant

good-smelling heads and goo-goo-ga-ga and (delicious) baby food for everyone. What it really meant was less of everything: time, attention, food, space . . .

"Wait," I said. "A baby needs a nursery."

"Yes," Mom said. "We'll pick out some new paint when we swing by Homer's later today."

"Nontoxic, of course," Dad said with a grin. "It'll be fun!"

Then I realized what they really meant.

"I'm not getting my own room," I said. It wasn't a question. It was a statement of absolute truth.

Mom looked at me all surprised, like it never occurred to her. "Oh! Oh, honey."

"But what about me?" Violet said.

"You can still have my office," Mom said. "As long as you don't mind my campaign stuff all over the dining room table."

Violet smiled and slipped her headphones back on.

Why did I ever think we were on the same team? Violet was on *their* team because *she* was still getting her own room. So much for the Older Sister Alliance. Second oldest meant next to nothing in this family.

"Dahlia, are you excited to move in with Clover?" Dad asked.

"You must be talking about some other Clover," I said. "Because you cannot be talking about me."

Dahlia squealed.

"Dahlia uses a heart nightlight projector," I said. "And she steals my art supplies."

"Is Dahlia going to jail?" Daisy asked.

"Maybe she should," I said.

"Find your filter, Clover," Dad warned me. He says that when I go too far or say something mean.

"Sorry," I said. Dahlia frowned, and I felt kind of bad. The new baby wasn't her fault. Sometimes when I talk without a filter, it hurts people's feelings. I'm good at a lot of things, like art. One thing I'm not good at is hiding my feelings.

But really, I don't think it's some big accomplishment if you're great at hiding your feelings. That's just more lying.

Mom turned around. I could see in her eyes that she was kind of sorry. But she also looked happy. Happy there was going to be more of us. But did anyone ask the kids who already existed what they wanted?

"Can you still run for school board when you're

pregnant?" Violet asked as we piled out of the van.

"Of course," Mom said. "But there's something we need to talk about before we go inside. The baby needs to be a secret for now."

Daisy gasped. "Secrets, secrets are no fun!" she said.

"Secrets, secrets hurt . . ." Dahlia said, pausing dramatically. "My buns!"

"It's *not* 'my buns'!" Daisy screamed. "It's '*some-one*.' Secrets, secrets hurt someone."

"There's a reason I want to keep it a secret," Mom said. "A couple of reasons, actually. I'm only eleven weeks along. That's on the early side, and we want to make sure the baby is healthy." She lowered her voice. "Also, politics can be . . . difficult."

"'Difficult' means 'hard,'" said Dahlia smugly.

"Some people might think that if I'm pregnant, I won't do a good job on the school board," Mom said.

"Why not?" Daisy asked.

Mom shrugged. "It's just old-fashioned thinking. That a woman can't work if she's raising a family or taking care of a baby. That's not true, and it's not fair. But that's the way some people feel. So can we agree to keep this a family secret for now?"

She made a *shhhh* sound with her finger up to her lips.

Dahlia and Daisy did the shush-finger thing like Mom. Juniper tried, too, but she just kind of spit.

"A secret?" I said. "Don't you mean a lie? Are you going to wear tents or something to hide it?" Dad gave me the "find your filter" face without saying a word.

Maybe hiding your pregnancy is better than whatever that guy who went to jail did. But Mom was lying, too. In a way, maybe her lie was worse because I had to keep her secret, and I was her kid. How is it okay to make your own kids lie when if they lie on their own, they get in trouble? And why is it okay to lie when you're an adult? I guess it's because you're the one who gives the punishments, and it's easy not to punish yourself.

We gathered Mom's campaign stuff from the trunk and headed to the Town Hall entrance. Dad hummed as Mom's cross-body bag flopped around on his hip.

Dad always hums as a way to change the subject, to move past bad feelings like they're not even there.

"Who's ready for pancakes?" Dad asked as he pushed open the door to Town Hall.

Everyone squealed except for Violet and me. Violet didn't squeal because she probably thought squealing was typical. But I didn't squeal because my heart was breaking. I wasn't getting my own room. My dreams were as important as the litter on the floor of our minivan.